HARD BARGAINING

"Welcome," said Blythe Donnen in a low, husky voice as she let Skye Fargo into her lavishly furnished house. She wore a floor-length, form-fitting white gown that made her black hair and eyebrows look almost painted. But what Skye noticed most was the row of buttons that went down the entire length of the front of her gown.

Blythe gestured to a tray on a round table. "Roast beef and bourbon," she said. "I thought you might be hungry."

"I am, but I was thinking of nibbling on something else," Fargo said.

Blythe's smile grew a fraction wider. Slowly she began to unbutton her gown, starting at the top and going down.

Blythe had invited Skye Fargo here to sweeten her offer to him—and every button opened made it look sweeter and sweeter. . . .

LONGHORN
GUNS

by

Jon Sharpe

Ⓞ
A SIGNET BOOK
NEW AMERICAN LIBRARY

PUBLISHER'S NOTE

This novel is a work of fiction. Names, characters, places, and incidents either are the product of the author's imagination or are used fictitiously, and any resemblance to actual persons, living or dead, events, or locales is entirely coincidental.

NAL BOOKS ARE AVAILABLE AT QUANTITY DISCOUNTS
WHEN USED TO PROMOTE PRODUCTS OR SERVICES.
FOR INFORMATION PLEASE WRITE TO PREMIUM MARKETING DIVISION.
NEW AMERICAN LIBRARY. 1633 BROADWAY.
NEW YORK. NEW YORK 10019.

Copyright © 1986 by Jon Sharpe

The first chapter of this book previously appeared in *Posse from Hell*, the fifty-second volume in this series.

SIGNET TRADEMARK REG. U.S. PAT. OFF. AND FOREIGN COUNTRIES
REGISTERED TRADEMARK—MARCA REGISTRADA
HECHO EN CHICAGO. U.S.A.

SIGNET, SIGNET CLASSIC, MENTOR, PLUME, MERIDIAN and NAL BOOKS are published by New American Library, 1633 Broadway, New York, New York 10019

First Signet Printing, May, 1986

1 2 3 4 5 6 7 8 9

PRINTED IN THE UNITED STATES OF AMERICA

The Trailsman

Beginnings . . . they bend the tree and they mark the man. Skye Fargo was born when he was eighteen. Terror was his midwife, vengeance his first cry. Killing spawned Skye Fargo, ruthless, cold-blooded murder. Out of the acrid smoke of gunpowder still hanging in the air, he rose, cried out a promise never forgotten.

The Trailsman, they began to call him, all across the West: searcher, scout, hunter, the man who could see where others only looked, his skills for hire but not his soul, the man who lived each day to the fullest, yet trailed each tomorrow. Skye Fargo, the Trailsman, the seeker who could take the wildness of a land and the wanting of a woman and make them his own.

*1861, the Colorado Territory,
where the San Juan Mountains spilled
into New Mexico, and the greed
and blood of men followed. . . .*

1

He didn't want company.

He didn't need company.

He didn't expect company.

And he sure as hell didn't figure on the voice that shouted through the closed door of the little room. "Open up, dammit," the voice roared. "That's my wife you've got in there, mister."

Skye Fargo turned lake-blue eyes on the young woman in the bed with him. She had just shed the last of her clothes and sat naked in front of him, smallish but nicely shaped breasts, rounded hips, a tiny belly that curved down to a modest black triangle. "What the hell's all this about?" Fargo half-whispered as he stared hard at the pale-blue eyes in a round, slightly vacant face. The girl lifted one shoulder in a shrug and one small breast rose with the motion.

"You hear me in there?" the voice shouted from the hallway. "Come out, and your hands better be the only thing up."

Fargo swung from the bed and drew clothes over his powerfully muscled body, his eyes still on the girl in the bed. "You never said a damn thing about any husband," he accused.

9

She shrugged again, and Fargo stepped to the window of the old, frame hotel as he buckled on his gun belt. He had a second-floor room, and he saw two men below the window, looking up, and a third one at the far end of the narrow alleyway. His eyes were blue ice as they returned to the girl. He was at the bed in one long-legged stride. Grabbing a handful of dark-blond hair, he yanked her small, naked body to him. "Too quick, everybody in position. They had to be ready and waiting. Something stinks, honey. You set me up for this," he hissed.

Her pale-blue eyes grew round with fear.

"Open up or we start shootin'," the voice called from outside the door.

Fargo flung the girl back, and she bounced on the bed. His mouth had drawn itself into a thin line. There had to be a rear exit from the old hotel. But that meant getting out of the room, and he'd detected more than one pair of footsteps outside the door. "Break it open," the voice outside roared.

"I'd get under the bed, doll," Fargo said quietly, and saw a flash of white, round rump as the girl rolled from the bed and started to crawl beneath it. Fargo darted across the room, flattened himself against the wall beside the door, the big Colt in hand as the volley of shots blew the latch out of the old wood.

The door flew open and three figures rushed in, spraying the room with wild gunfire. As they halted midway into the room, Fargo fired one shot, and the figure nearest him clutched at his thigh as he fell with a yelp of pain. The other two dived for the floor but Fargo spun, catapulted himself through the opened door and into the hallway. He saw a stairway leading down at the rear end of the hallway, raced for it just as two men came up the steps.

He swung the barrel of the Colt in a flat arc,

10

crashed it into the first man's temple, and the man toppled backward, slamming into the figure behind him, who went down on one knee. Fargo took the top steps two at a time, vaulted over the two figures sprawled there, and raced down the stairs. He saw the rear door, hit it with his shoulder at full speed, and half-flew out of the hotel. He spied the two figures nearby at once, and hit the ground, rolling as the two men yanked guns. The Trailsman fired as he rolled and saw one figure go down and the other fling himself sideways. Leaping to his feet, he raced around the rear corner of the hotel and streaked for the hitching post outside the front entrance, where his horse was tethered. He skidded around the front corner of the old hotel and dropped to a crouch. Three men were positioned by his horse: two in front of the striking black-and-white Ovaro, one by the hitching post.

Too damn many men, Fargo swore inwardly. This was no irate husband keeping tabs on his little wife. He'd been set up. He swore as he backed down the narrow space alongside the hotel. He started to run and saw three men race around the rear corner and halt to fire. Fargo fired first, and one whirled as he fell. Fargo dropped on one knee as a hail of bullets hurtled over his head, fired again as his marksmanship sent another figure sprawling with a cry of pain.

Just then he heard the other three men that had been beside the Ovaro race up. He'd be trapped in a cross fire. He swore as he tried to flatten himself against the wall of the building.

The horse and rider seemed to appear out of nowhere, charging at a full gallop out of the dark shadows beyond the rear of the hotel. Fargo stayed against the wall as the rider raced into the narrow alleyway, a wide-brimmed, floppy, battered hat

11

obscuring the rider's face, a loose buckskin jacket blowing in the wind. The rider skidded the horse, a roan gelding, to a halt, motioned, and Fargo vaulted onto the horse in back of the figure in the saddle. Half-turning as the rider sent the horse streaking from the alleyway, Fargo fired two shots back at the three men that appeared, and watched them duck away. The horseman swerved the roan into tree cover beyond the edge of the small town, kept the horse at a full gallop until they were well into the trees.

"Whoa, there," Fargo said. "This is far enough." The rider reined to a halt, and Fargo slid to the ground. "I sure owe you one, friend," he said, and bent forward to peer up under the wide-brimmed, floppy hat. He glimpsed a young face, unlined and smooth-cheeked.

The rider whisked off the hat. "I'll save you time looking and wondering," the horseman said, and Fargo felt the frown dig into his brow.

"I'll be dammed," he murmured as he stared at the blond hair pulled up high into a bun. "You're a girl." A damn pretty one, he added silently as he took in a long, graceful neck, even features, a short, straight nose, well-shaped lips, strong but nicely molded chin, and eyes he couldn't decide the color of in the darkness.

"Get back on. We've ground to cover. They'll be coming after you," she said.

"Not till I get my horse," Fargo answered.

"Your horse?" She frowned.

"He's a very special horse," Fargo said.

A look of tight-lipped annoyance hardened her pretty features. "I didn't save your neck so you could go back and get yourself killed," she snapped.

"Just why did you save it?" Fargo questioned.

"I've my reasons," she said stiffly.

12

"Who are you?" he asked.

"Get back on, and let's get away from here," she said, ignoring his question.

"Sorry," Fargo said. "I'm real beholden to you, but I'm going back for my Ovaro."

"You're a damn fool," she said angrily.

"Maybe, but I'm going to be a damn fool with his horse," Fargo said. "Thanks again. Maybe we'll be meeting again sometime."

He turned and set off through the trees in a long-legged trot, and she stayed in place on her roan. She was right, he realized. They'd be looking for him, whoever they were. But he guessed they wouldn't figure him to return for his horse, and he increased his speed as he put aside questions that jabbed at him about the blond girl.

The buildings of the town came into sight, and he ran on with his eyes narrowed. The town had a name, Ten Rocks, and he'd stopped there to relax after a long day's riding. But instead of relaxing in a warm bed with a warm girl, he found himself set up, turned into a target, and rescued by a rider out of the night that turned out to be a lovely blonde.

It had turned into one hell of a strange night, he grunted as he slowed when the dingy white structure of the hotel loomed up behind the end of the trees. He moved along the edge of the treeline at an angle that brought him opposite the front of the hotel. He saw the Ovaro still tethered to the hitching post, and held back the impulse to race across the open ground to the horse. Instead, he let his eyes slowly move across the doorway of the hotel and probe into the deep shadows at the sides of the building. He found the figure standing in the shadows at the entrance to the alleyway beside the hotel. The man held a rifle in his hands as he peered out from the alleyway. Fargo swore silently again. He had underestimated them. They'd seen that the Ovaro was not the kind of horse a man left behind. And that meant the rifleman wasn't alone. They were wily, and they wouldn't leave one man on guard without support.

His eyes were narrowed as he peered down along the darkened storefronts along Main Street. He couldn't discern any other figures in the blackness, but they were there, he was certain. He faded back along the treeline and worked his way around until he was across from the rear of the hotel. Keeping in a crouch, he darted across the dozen yards of open ground, a silent shadow in the night, halted when he reached the rear of the narrow alleyway. Moving slowly now, on steps silent and stealthy as a cougar on the hunt, he crept up the alleyway toward the rifleman at the other end.

Drawing the big Colt from its holster, he crept up behind the man who stared unaware out toward the hitching post. Fargo brought the butt of the gun down hard on the man's head, caught his sagging body with one hand and his rifle with the other before it clattered to the ground. He pulled the man back into the alleyway and lowered him to the ground, stepped back to the mouth of the alleyway, and peered out to the Ovaro at the hitching post. Only a few yards, he measured. The others wouldn't be watching the alleyway, but they'd see him when he raced out into the open. They'd have to see him, recover from their initial surprise, pull guns, and aim. He estimated he'd have maybe fifteen or twenty seconds' surprise advantage. Not much, but it'd have to be enough, he grunted.

He crouched, gathered himself, and sprang forward into a full run, his powerful leg muscles driving him across the few yards. He reached the Ovaro, flipped the reins from the hitching post with an out-stretched arm as he vaulted into the saddle. The shouts and shots came together, but he had already flattened himself over the horse's withers as he sent the Ovaro racing toward the trees. Staying flattened, he turned his head enough to see three riders come out from between buildings and start after him. He reached the trees, rode into the tall cottonwoods as he straightened in the saddle.

He heard the sound to his left and brought the Colt up and around to fire as he saw the horse and rider coming toward him. The rider's wide-brimmed, floppy hat flapped up and down, and he heard her call from beneath the outfit. "This way," she said, and swerved the roan up a steep incline through the trees. He fell in behind her. The incline grew steeper, and he felt the Ovaro pull hard.

The incline ended abruptly, and he saw the horse ahead of him swerve sharply left and race into a nar-row rock-lined passage. He followed, saw the horse turn into a side passageway equally narrow. He drew closer and was almost at her tail when she brought the roan out of the passage into a series of rolling hills. He followed as she sent the roan full out until the land dipped and he saw the shack at the bottom of a small hollow, the dim moon strong enough for him to see a sagging roof. The road halted at the little cabin, and the rider pulled the floppy, battered hat off and once again Fargo was struck by the even-featured pretti-ness of the girl. He still couldn't make out the color of her eyes.

"You can hole up in here till morning," the girl said. "I'll be leaving now."

"Hold it, honey, not so fast," Fargo protested as she began to turn the roan. "I don't even know who to thank. Who are you?"

"Nobody," she said crisply.

"You can do better than that," Fargo said as he slid from the Ovaro.

"Be more careful from now on," she said, again ignoring his remark.

"You can't just ride off," Fargo said. "You were waiting. You knew about it. Why was I set up?"

Her glance grew disapproving as the line of her chin stiffened. "It was part your fault," she said.

"My fault?" He frowned in protest.

"If you hadn't been so damn eager for a little piece of easy ass, they couldn't have trapped you like that." She sniffed disdainfully.

She had a sharp tongue, he grunted silently. And she was right, of course, he added with a bitter taste in his mouth. "That still doesn't answer my question. Why was I set up?" he asked.

Disdain remained in the gaze she fastened on him. "Ask yourself," she snapped.

"What the hell does that mean?"

"You know who you are. You know where you're going," she threw back at him, and she all but disappeared under the wide-brimmed, floppy hat she jammed over her blond hair. She slapped the roan on the rump and the horse surged forward.

"Wait! Will I be seeing you again?" Fargo called after her.

"No," she said, not looking back.

Fargo frowned into the night after her as she vanished into the trees.

2

Fargo turned away and went into the shack to see a bunk bed outlined in the moonlight that streamed through the doorway. He undressed, slipped the latch bolt in place on the door, and stretched out on the lower bunk as he tried to sort out all that had happened. A few of the pieces fell into place, but too damn few, he grunted. First, he wondered how they'd known he'd be in Ten Rocks, but that answered itself as he thought more about it. Ten Rocks was the only town on the way to Mountainville, another full day's ride. Logic dictated he'd be stopping there. All of which meant that whoever they were, they knew he was on his way to Mountainville.

Whoever they were, Fargo frowned, and immediately thought about the hard-riding blonde that had appeared out of the night clothed in a man's outfit. She had to have known too, and she had a talent for cryptic answers that intimated he ought to know why he'd been set up and made into a target. Only she'd been all wrong there. He hadn't any idea why, and he thought back to when he'd agreed to go to Mountainville. It had been outside Rock Springs in the Wyoming Territory when the man had come to him and introduced himself as Aaron Highbard. A narrow-framed man, he said he'd been sent by a group of independent cattle ranchers who wanted a new trail blazed into Albuquerque. Fargo had told Aaron Highbard he'd another small job to finish first, and the man had agreed they'd wait for him. The agreement had been sealed with a payment of traveling money and a handshake.

That's all there had been, nothing more than a routine agreement for a routine job of trailblazing. Only now it suddenly seemed a lot more than routine, and he decided another visit to Ten Rocks might bring some answers. He wouldn't look for the men. They'd been virtually faceless figures in the darkness, and he wouldn't recognize any of them if he met them face to face. But if they were still there, they'd spot him and the Ovaro. They'd likely try again for him, and that's what he wanted, another chance at getting his hands on one of them. But there were two faces he'd very much recognize. One belonged to the pale-eyed little sneak that had set him up, and the other to the very pretty, even-featured blond rescuer out of the night. He'd search for both and be content to find either one.

He finally let himself sleep. The night stayed quiet until it fled with the morning sun and he woke with the new day. He found a stream near the shack, washed, dressed and breakfasted on thorn apples as he headed the Ovaro down through the rocky passages back toward town. His thoughts returned to the pale-eyed girl he had met outside the hotel and how she used her admiration of the Ovaro as a way to start a conversation. She hadn't wasted any time with the rest of it, letting him know that she was new and lonely in town and that she'd welcome company. She'd been clever, almost bold, but not quite, giving out all the right signals. Another voice intruded into his recollection, and he felt his lips draw back in a wry grimace. "If you hadn't been so damn eager for a little piece of easy ass . . ." it said. The truth stung. He clicked off thoughts as Ten Rocks came into sight.

He rode slowly down Main Street and halted at the dance hall. Hitching the horse loosely, he stepped inside, halted, scanned the eight girls as they break-fasted at round wooden tables, some with their hair tied in ribbons, most without lipstick or makeup, all with tired eyes.

"We're not open yet, big boy," an older woman said, and Fargo scanned the girls again.

"Got any others?" he asked.

"Now, this is no time to go judging my girls," the woman bristled.

"I'm not judging, I'm asking," Fargo said coldly, and the woman wiped the resentment from her face.

"No," she said.

Fargo nodded back and left the dance hall. He believed the woman. He'd seen no flicker of alarm or caution in her, and he slowly swung back onto the striking black-and-white horse. As he did so, he spied two figures shrink back into a doorway across the street from the dance hall. Giving no sign that he'd seen them, he slowly turned the Ovaro and headed out of town. He rode casually, staying on the road that curved out of the south end of the town. He didn't so much as glance back. He had no need to do so. They'd be following, maybe with others, hanging back, being careful for now. They had seen the Ovaro, of course, and had waited in the doorway.

He drifted from the road when the low hills rose and made straight for a tall box elder that stood by itself in full-branched splendor. Halting under the tree, he dismounted, stretched his long frame out on the grass, resting his head against the grayish-brown, thin bark at the base of the thick trunk. He pushed his hat down over his face, folded both hands across his chest, and became a man hard asleep in the cool shade of the big tree. But beneath the hands folded across his chest, the big Colt lay flat, his finger resting against the trigger.

He waited, even closed his eyes, letting his ears tell him when he had company. Opening his eyes into a slit, he could see out from under the brim of the hat. The two men hadn't gathered any others but had dismounted as they moved stealthily toward him, their horses left halfway down the gentle hillside. Fargo stayed motionless, watching them draw closer until they stood in front of him. Through his slitted gaze he saw that one wore a torn stetson, the other a cut-down sombrero. Under their hats, both men had the ferretlike expressions of perpetual drifters, and he cursed inwardly as he saw them start to reach for their guns. He'd hoped they'd say something first, anything that might furnish a clue to what this was all about. But they weren't going to do that, and he was ready, expecting the worst, the Colt under his folded hands already turned, aimed.

He fired two shots so fast they sounded as though they were one. The one at the right clutched at his hand as his gun flew into the air while the other one looked down to see a bullet hit the butt of the gun half out of the holster and send the pistol end over end. Both men froze in place. They stared at Fargo as he sat up and slid his hat back atop his head.

"You two could be dead now," Fargo said slowly. "The only reason you're not is because I want some answers." He pushed himself to his feet as the two men continued to stare at him, hands half raised in

20

the air. "Why was I set up?" Fargo thrust at them sharply.

"We don't know," the one wearing the torn stetson said.

Fargo pulled the hammer back on the big Colt. "I don't have time for more games," he said evenly.

"That's the truth. We don't know," the man blurted out.

"Honest we don't," the other one added.

The Colt barked once as Fargo pulled the trigger, and the one with the cut-down sombrero clutched at his face in pain as the top of his ear disappeared. "Ow, shit," he screamed.

"I'll ask one more time. Why?"

"Christ, don't shoot. We don't know, dammit," the torn stetson said, and cringed. The other one had fallen to one knee, his hand held to his ear as he pressed a kerchief to the side of his face.

"Somebody hired you and the others," Fargo growled.

"He never told us why. He just gave everybody their instructions. That's all he said," the drifter answered.

Fargo shifted the Colt a fraction and fired again. The torn stetson flew from the man's head, and a tiny trickle of blood coursed down from the edge of his hairline. "The next one's going to be right between your eyes," Fargo said matter-of-factly.

"Dammit, mister, we can't tell you anything more. We don't know anything more," the man screamed in fear. "He just hired us. He didn't tell us why."

"He have a name?" Fargo questioned.

"Eddie. He called himself Eddie, nothing else," the man said.

"What about the girl?" Fargo asked.

"He hired her, too—had her with him when he came to town," the man said.

Fargo shifted the Colt a fraction and fastened a glare at the other man still on one knee. The man cringed in terror at once. "No, I don't know anything else. We're tellin' you the truth, we don't know more," he cried out.

Fargo peered hard at him, shifted his eyes to peer hard at the torn stetson's fear-filled face. Small scum, strictly for hire, he reckoned. They were probably telling the truth. They were scared out of their wits, and they'd surely talk if they knew anything. They weren't the kind to be martyrs. "Where's the girl now?" he asked.

"Left last night after she was paid, like everybody else," the man said.

"Why'd you two stay in town?" Fargo queried.

"We got in on an all-night poker game," the man said.

"When we saw the horse, we figured we could get another bankroll if we brought you in," the other said, still pressing his ear.

"In where?" Fargo flared, and raised his Colt. "You just told me you didn't know anything more. You've been lying, you weasels. But it'll be for the last time."

"No, don't shoot," the torn stetson screamed in panic. "We didn't lie. After it all went wrong last night, Eddie said he'd stop outside town today."

"Why?" Fargo frowned.

The man licked his lips, quickly glancing at the other one, who'd lifted himself to his feet. "He said he'd pay extra if anybody spotted you," the torn stetson said.

"And you two got lucky," Fargo added grimly, and the man half-shrugged almost apologetically. "You were going to bring me in and get a real bonus. Where's your friend Eddie going to be?"

"This side of town, alongside the road," the man said.

"When?" Fargo snapped.

"Noon," the man answered.

Fargo cast a quick glance at the sun. It was almost in the noon sky, and his thoughts raced for a moment. "Get your horses," he said. "We don't want to disappoint Eddie."

The two men frowned at him as he followed them down the gentle slope to where they'd left their horses. The torn stetson picked up his hat along the way, and Fargo holstered his own Colt and scooped up the two guns he'd shot out of their hands. He held one in each hand as he swung onto the Ovaro and watched the two men mount their horses.

"You're going to bring me in," Fargo said. "Eddie will be real happy to see you."

The two drifters exchanged quick glances, he saw as he moved the Ovaro in between their horses. He folded both arms across his chest, a gun in each hand tucked under each crossed arm.

"Move out," he ordered. "When Eddie sees us coming, it's going to look just like you're bringing me in. He'll even think you've got my arms tied. Only we know that I've a gun pointed at each of you. One wrong move and I shoot."

Both men nodded as he rode slowly forward between them. They reached the roadway at the bottom of the gentle slope and wheeled left and back toward Ten Rocks. Fargo cast another glance at the two drifters on either side of him as he rode with arms folded. The fear was gone from their faces, and Fargo frowned. Something was wrong. They were suddenly too damn calm. Yet they had to know they couldn't try anything. All he had to do was pull the triggers. At this range he couldn't miss. He threw another quick glance at both men as they continued to ride beside him with sudden calm. Maybe they were just relieved to be alive, he pondered, but the uneasiness stayed with him.

He slowed as he spied the lone horseman standing quietly at a bend in the road. Ten Rocks was a hazy outline in the distance. "Is that him?" Fargo muttered, and the torn stetson nodded. "Don't do anything stupid," Fargo warned as he saw the man turn his horse to face the three riders approaching. Fargo's eyes grew ice blue as he moved steadily toward the man. There was no way for the man to see or think anything other than what it seemed to be, the two hired guns bringing him in. But suddenly Fargo saw the man reach one hand to his side. Almost in disbelief, he saw Eddie bring his gun up.

"Goddamn!" Fargo breathed. There was no time to wonder why. There wasn't even time to unfold his arms. There was only time to press the triggers of the two guns as he fell forward over the Ovaro's sturdy neck. He heard the sound of bullets hissing over his head and saw the two drifters topple from their horses. But Eddie raced his horse forward as he fired again, and Fargo let himself slip around the far side of the Ovaro's neck and drop to the ground. He landed on both feet in a low crouch, slapped the horse on the rump, and the Ovaro ran forward. He saw Eddie bringing his horse around for another charge. The man saw the Ovaro surge on, spotted the crouched figure that appeared from behind the horse, and tried to bring his gun down. He was too late as Fargo fired both guns at once. The two shots struck the man full in the chest, and he seemed to explode in a shower of red. He toppled backward over the rump of his horse and hit the ground with the dull thudding sound of a lifeless body.

"Dammit," Fargo bit out as he straightened up. Eddie wouldn't be telling him anything. He glanced at the two drifters, who lay on the ground nearby. One was still, his side a spreading stain of dark red. However, the torn stetson was alive, Fargo saw, sitting up with both hands clutched to his leg.

"The thigh bone's broken," the man moaned as Fargo stepped over to him. He yanked the man's head up, his ice-blue eyes still furious.

"How did he know?" Fargo demanded. "He couldn't have seen anything. How did he know, goddammit?" He pushed the gun into the man's face, and the man swallowed hard.

"He told us all last night that he wanted you brought in dead, no other way but dead," the man gasped out.

"Damn," Fargo snapped. That explained it, of course. When the man saw the two drifters bringing him back alive, he knew something was wrong. It explained why the two drifters had grown so calm so suddenly. They saw the tables being turned, certain Eddie would respond exactly the way he had. Fargo threw the two guns into the nearby brush and walked to the Ovaro. "I wouldn't waste another bullet on you," he said as he climbed onto the horse.

"My leg's splintered and bleedin' bad. You can't leave me here," the drifter protested.

"You're the lucky one. You can crawl," Fargo said as he put the pinto into a canter. He rode on, turned, skirted the town, and made his way along the low hills. Two more dead, another close call, and he still knew no more than he did last night. The answers had to lay in Mountainville, and he headed south as the tall peaks of the San Juan Mountains rose at his right. He rode steadily but unhurriedly. He'd lost too much time to make Mountainville before dark, and there was no need for hurrying now.

The gently rolling hill country bordered good, flat plains with the San Juan range close by to his right. Far away to the left, beyond the horizon line, lay the peaks of the Sangre de Cristo Mountains. In between the two ranges, the flatland was rich and lush. This was Cheyenne country, with a good sprinkling of Kiowa and some Kansas. But it was the Cheyenne who laid claim to the mountains and the flatland below. They still roamed and raided the plains and plateaus, but they'd moved most of their big camps into the mountains and away from the guns and eyes of the bluecoats. From the foothills, they could raid as they pleased, command the land, and be secure behind the natural barriers of the mountains.

The Kiowa stayed mostly on the vast plains as they swept in from the east, but Kiowa strayed far and wide. Occasionally the Apache would venture up from New Mexico. But it was the Cheyenne warriors that left their marks across the land where he rode, unshod ponies, a piece of torn wrist gauntlet, the remains of a small trail fire that had used the birch-bark tinder they favored. He had been given directions by Aaron Highbard, and as the day began to wear down, he pulled the slip of paper from his pocket and read aloud from it as he rode: "Past Mountainville, first right through a double row of staghorn sumac. Double Z Ranch." He tucked the paper back into his pocket and kept the pinto at a fast trot through rising hills lush with greenery and covered with thick stands of tanbark oak, shadbush, and white birch.

He had just reached a line of shadbush at the top of a low hill when he heard the gunshots. He slowed the pinto and swerved the horse into the trees as he gazed down at the next hill. He saw the two riders racing up the hillside at an angle, their horses full out. Another burst of gunfire brought his eyes to the top of the hill where three more horsemen came into sight. They were plainly chasing somebody, and suddenly the lone horseman burst into view, battered, wide-brimmed hat flopping in the wind, jacket drawn tight.

"I'll be damned," Fargo muttered as his gaze stayed on the unmistakable rider. She was outracing the three pursuers behind her, but the two nearly at the top of the hill now would cut her off. They'd have her sandwiched between them in moments.

Fargo pulled the big Sharps out of its saddle holster and put it to his shoulder. Unwilling to shoot to kill without knowing anything more about the chase, he took careful aim, fired, and one of the two riders nearing the top of the hill reined up as the shot creased his shirt. Fargo fired again, and the second man's mount reared up as the shot passed between his ears. Fargo swung the rifle toward the three other pursuers, fired, and saw the trio break ranks and peel off. His gaze went to the battered, wide-brimmed hat as, head bent low, she swept into the trees and was gone.

He lowered the rifle and stayed motionless as the five pursuers wheeled their horses, peered across the hillside in the fading light. They had lost their quarry, they realized, and they milled about for a few minutes before finally riding away together. They had come from the bottom of the hills, and as Fargo put the Sharps into its holster, he sent the Ovaro slowly down-ward. He rode a zigzag pattern down the hillside in the remaining light of the day until he saw the road below and the wagon with one side rider. He headed for the wagon and saw a big dead-axle dray with chain-linked stake sides and extra diagonal braces for the rear wheels. A short-horned yearling bull filledthe wagon, and Fargo saw the two men raise rifles as he came toward them.

"That's far enough, mister," the driver said.

"Just came down to see if you were all right. I heard all the shooting," Fargo said.

"We are now, but we were almost bushwhacked," the driver said, and Fargo moved the pinto closer as the men lowered their rifles some.

"Almost?" he echoed.

"They were waiting for us when a feller in a loose jacket and a big, floppy, wide-brimmed hat flushed them out, came racing down shooting into the trees where they were hiding," the wagon driver said. "Eb and me, we started shooting, and they decided to take off after the feller that flushed them out."

"He got away, I saw him," Fargo said.

"That's good. We're obliged to him," the man said.

"Why'd they try to bushwhack you?" Fargo queried.

"I'd guess to get Ruth Larkin's young bull back in the wagon," the side rider answered. "He was at Doc Fisher's for a few days to be checked out. We were just bringing him back. Ruth Larkin figures he'll be the heart of her new herd."

"You know who they were?" Fargo asked.

The man on the wagon made a wry sound. "Hell, there's so much bad blood around here you could point at damn near anybody," he said. "Thanks for coming down to see. We'll be gettin' on now."

Fargo nodded and moved the pinto back as the wagon began to roll forward. He stayed until the wagon was out of sight and the night silently descended. He walked the pinto toward Mountainville as he thought about the figure under the floppy, wide-brimmed hat. What the hell was she, he wondered, a strange girl who got her kicks running around doing good deeds, playing Robin Hood in disguise? He shook away the description. It didn't fit. This was the second time she'd been at the right place at the right moment. More than coincidence, he grunted, and more than aimless good deeds. She knew something, and she was striking back in her own way. But why? And what for?

He was sure of one thing only. She hadn't seen him. She hadn't had time to do anything but race away, and she was probably wondering who had given her the chance to escape. He shook his head as he rode on. This trip wasn't getting any less surprising, he frowned, and he put the pinto into a trot as the dark shape of a town came into sight.

Mountainville had its name over the closed general store and the wide-open saloon, he noted as he rode down Main Street. It was a larger town than Ten Rocks, with its own bank, stage depot, and a modest church. He rode on through town. The night was still young, and his mind still full of questions for Aaron Highbard. He stayed on the road that wound its way out of the other end of Mountainville and finally spotted the double row of staghorn sumac. A narrow road branched off to the right between the trees, and he took it until it ended where a small ranch house and two corrals spread out.

Lights were on in the house, and the door opened as Fargo rode to a halt. Aaron Highbard stepped out, his narrow frame silhouetted in the light from the doorway, a rifle in his hands. He lowered the gun when he noted the Ovaro. "Fargo, by God," the man said with both warmth and surprise in his voice. "Come in. Didn't expect you'd be arriving by night."

"Me neither," Fargo grunted as he followed the man into a modest house where everything looked a little worn. A woman with graying hair and a tired face that nonetheless managed to look pleasant came out of the kitchen.

"Martha, this is Fargo, the Trailsman," Aaron Highbard introduced, and Fargo nodded at the woman.

"I just stopped by," he said. "Got a few questions."

"Have a good trip?" Aaron Highbard said as he set the rifle down in a corner of the room.

"It was interesting," Fargo commented dryly. "I was set up once and almost killed three times." He saw the man's brows lift. "I got the idea that it all had something to do with my coming here," Fargo went on, deciding not to mention the blond rescuer. His eyes bored into Aaron Highbard, and he saw the man swallow as his wife faded out of the room silently. "Maybe you'd like to tell me I'm wrong?" Fargo pushed at him, and Aaron Highbard looked uncomfortable.

"Look, you can meet all the others tomorrow morning," the man said. "Ruth Larkin will explain everything then."

Fargo felt his brows lower at the man. "Ruth Larkin?" he echoed.

"She sort of heads up our group," Aaron Highbard said.

"Some bushwhackers tried to get that young bull calf of hers a little while back," Fargo said, and Aaron's eyes widened in surprise. "I still want some answers," Fargo said.

"Tomorrow morning. I'll see that everybody's here," the man said.

"It seems that a lot of people know you hired me," Fargo remarked.

"It was talked about. We never meant it to be a secret," Aaron said. "Ruth will explain it all to you."

Fargo's mouth tightened, but he nodded reluctantly. "I suppose a few hours more won't make any difference. But I get straight answers then or you get yourself somebody else," he warned.

"You'll get them," the man promised as Fargo walked from the house and swung onto the Ovaro. He rode away without glancing back, his mouth still tight, a knot of resentment growing inside him. It was plain he'd been told less than the whole truth when he'd been hired, but he was going to give them the doubt until morning. Maybe things had changed after Aaron Highbard had hired him.

He turned his thoughts to the blond rider out of the night. She had rescued him and interrupted the attempt to steal the yearling bull. Was she part of the independent ranchers' group? She sure seemed to be helping their cause, whatever it was. But then, why had she refused to tell him anything, even her name? She continued to be a woman of mystery, and he wondered when she might pop up again as he rode back to Mountainville and pulled up in front of the saloon. Whiskey had a way of loosening men's tongues, and a saloon was a good place to pick up all kinds of stray pieces of information.

He entered, scanned the place, and found a very ordinary saloon—no girls, no piano players, a dozen bare wood tables, some taken up by card players, and a long, nicked and battered bar. He stepped to the bar, ordered bourbon, and got a glass of something that only nodded in the direction of good drink. He had taken his third, slow sip, his ears tuned to the conversations around him, when he heard the man's voice lift in a taunting half-snarl.

"Only men drink at this bar," the man said, and Fargo half-turned to get a better look at the speaker. He saw a big, burly man with a beefy, bullying face that held small eyes over a flattened nose. "Get outa here, fleashit," the man said, and Fargo noticed the slightly built youth at the bar, not much over eighteen years old, he guessed. The boy nursed a beer and tried to ignore the big, beefy-faced man.

But the man wasn't about to be ignored, and his voice grew louder. "I said get your yellow little ass outa here," he bellowed, and took a step toward the youth.

The boy looked up, and Fargo saw he was trying to summon up courage. "I don't want any trouble. I'm not bothering you, Johnson," the youth said.

"You're here. That bothers me. And you're one of those steershit independent ranchers. Get out," the man ordered.

Fargo saw a small man move, tug at the beefy-faced one's sleeve. "Take it easy, Harry. You know the boss said not to make trouble," he muttered.

"Simmons is too damn careful. I'm going to teach this little bastard not to come around here with real men," the one called Harry roared, and started for the boy.

The youth stood up, backed a few feet along the bar as Fargo saw the other patrons scatter. "I'm not looking for trouble. Leave me be, Johnson," the youth said.

"You're not tellin' me what to do," the burly figure bellowed. He lashed out, surprisingly quick, Fargo noted, and though the youth tried to duck away, the blow caught him alongside the face. It knocked him half around and he slammed into the bar and half-slid, half-fell to his knees.

"Don't, Harry," the smaller man said.

"Shut up," Harry Johnson snapped as he stepped forward, kicked out, and sunk his boot into the youth's ribs. The boy fell sideways with a grunt of pain. "I'm gonna bust him up good."

Harry Johnson plainly enjoyed winning no-contest

fights, his bullying ways reinforced by every uneven contest. Fargo had seen many like him, too many. "That's enough," he said just loud enough to be heard. "Leave him alone."

The big, beefy-faced figure, one fist upraised, turned and focused on the big man with the lake-blue eyes, the only figure still at the bar. "You say that?" he demanded.

"Seems that way," Fargo said, and took another sip of his bourbon.

Harry Johnson stared, disbelief in his beefy face. "Who the hell are you?" he roared.

"Name's Fargo. Skye Fargo."

Harry Johnson paused and an evil smile slid across his face. "Well, now, you're the Trailsman, the one those shitheads hired. Is that why you want to save this little shit's hide?" he growled.

"No, I just don't like bigmouthed bullying bastards," Fargo said, his tone almost weary.

Harry Johnson's eyes widened. "You're goin' to find out what I am," he raged, and threw a hard right.

Fargo pulled back and the blow grazed his face. He shot a short, straight left that landed in the burly figure's stomach, and Harry Johnson doubled over as he grunted in pain. Fargo crossed a right in an upward arc, but the man twisted away and the blow only scraped along his jaw.

"Son of a bitch," Johnson roared as he came back swinging with both arms.

Fargo parried the first two blows, weaved away from another two, and brought up a hard uppercut. It landed only halfway on Johnson's chin but with enough force to send him staggering backward. Fargo tried to follow through, but again the burly figure's quickness surprised him as Johnson ducked to avoid the blow. The man lowered his head and charged, bull-like, swinging both arms before him, and Fargo danced out onto the center of the saloon floor and parried and avoided the lunging blows. Johnson paused, lifted his head from behind his arms to take new aim at his opponent as Fargo's left shot out with lightninglike speed. The blow caught Johnson over the eye and instantly split his skin. A cascade of blood began to course down the left side of the man's face.

With a roar of rage, Johnson charged again, but this time, as he stepped to one side, Fargo drove a whistling uppercut in an upward arc. It caught Johnson along the side of the jaw and the man halted just long enough for Fargo's roundhouse left to smash into his chin. Johnson staggered back and his hands dropped. Fargo's looping right smashed full into the man's jaw, and Harry Johnson's feet crossed and he went down, landing on his face, and lay still.

Fargo stepped back, rubbed the knuckles of his right hand against his shirtfront, and met the young man's grateful gaze.

"I'm real obliged. He'd might have killed me," the youth said.

"My pleasure," Fargo said. He started to turn away when his ears picked up the sound behind him, the scrape of boot heels on the floor. He spun around and saw Johnson half on his feet as he yanked the gun from his holster.

"Bastard," the man cursed through lips that dripped blood. Fargo's hand moved with the speed of a diamondback's strike as the big Colt flew into his hand. He fired as Johnson's finger started to pull the trigger, two shots that plowed into the burly figure. Harry Johnson flew back as the first shot hit, then jerked convulsively on the floor as the second heavy bullet struck until, with surprising suddenness, his beefy face sagged into a battered, flabby, and lifeless mask.

Fargo turned to the small man who'd tried to dissuade Johnson from starting a fight. "He should've listened to you," Fargo commented as he stepped to the bar, picked up his glass, and drained the last of the bourbon. " 'Evening, gents," he said as he walked from the saloon, the small man staring at him with awe in his eyes. Fargo went outside, untied the Ovaro, and walked the horse down the street. He had noted a modest, gray wood house when he first rode through town and now he halted before the sign that read: HENSEN—OVERNIGHT BOARDERS.

Hensen turned out to be a formidable-looking woman, big-framed, with greying hair and piercing eyes in a face deeply lined with hard yesterdays. "Pay in advance," she said before she handed him the key to a first-floor room. "I run a respectful house, young feller," she added sternly.

He turned the word in his mind. "Respectful," he echoed. "What's that mean?"

"It means I don't care what you do so long as you do it quietly," she said.

"Fair enough." He grinned. "But I don't plan to do anything but sleep." He went down the hall, found the room, and latched the door. He undressed and stretched across the bed, more tired than he'd realized. But the events of the evening kept him from sleep. The young kid in the saloon would be running back with tales to tell. So would Harry Johnson's little sidekick, and another name had surfaced: Simmons. Tomorrow ought to bring him all the answers he wanted, from one direction or another, he contemplated. He finally closed away thoughts and sank into sleep.

3

He allowed himself to sleep later than usual. When he rose, he washed, dressed, and found coffee, bacon, and biscuits were being served in a small dining room. He breakfasted and went outside to the Ovaro, headed for the town stable. Using their body brush, stable sponge, and his own curry, he groomed the horse and then had his shoes checked. When he rode from the stable, the Ovaro's jet-black fore and hind quarters glistened and the pure white midsection seemed made of snow.

Fargo had just started from town when the two riders crossed in front of him and halted. He recognized one as the small man who'd been with Johnson in the saloon. The other horseman rode a handsome bay, a tall man with graying temples, handsome with an even-featured face that seemed to work hard at appearing strong.

" 'Morning," the man said. "I'm Howard Simmons. Been looking to spot that Ovaro of yours. You don't see many like that. Jack, here, told me about last night at the saloon. I want to apologize for that. Johnson disobeyed my orders."

"He paid for it," Fargo remarked.

"So he did," Simmons agreed, and his mouth formed a wry smile. The man wore a fine, embroidered shirt and equally fine riding trousers, Fargo noted. "Look, I'm having a little affair at my place tonight. I'd like you to come," Simmons said.

"Why?" Fargo asked.

"I'm president of the Mountainville Cattlemen's Combine. I'd like you to meet my associates. We'd like to tell you our side of things," Simmons explained.

Fargo sorted words in his mind. The man obviously thought he knew more than he did, and he decided to keep it that way for now. "I always like to hear both sides of anything," he answered.

"Good, then I'll expect you. My place is due south, where plains country starts. You can't miss it. Anytime after seven," Howard Simmons said. Fargo nodded, and the man turned the handsome bay and rode off with the smaller man at his side.

It was time to pay Aaron Highbard another visit, Fargo figured as he rode down the road from town, turned at the double row of sumacs until he reached the modest ranch. He found four buckboards and half a dozen horses outside, and the front door of the house opened as he rode up. Fargo swung from the saddle as those inside the house poured out, Aaron Highbard in the lead.

Fargo's gaze swept the men and women, some with youngsters, who gathered before him. They were an assorted lot, and he spottted the youth that had been in the saloon the night before. He searched for a pretty, even-featured blonde with hair piled atop her head, but there was no one that even resembled her. A woman stepped forward, brown hair pulled back straight. She had a strong face, pleasant more than pretty. In her late thirties, he guessed, with full, round breasts and a square-shouldered, sturdy shape.

Her brown eyes fixed a direct gaze at him as a youngster, about fourteen years old, came up to stand beside her.

"I'm Ruth Larkin," she said. "This is my son, Jess." Fargo nodded back. "We all heard of what happened at the saloon last night. I thank you for everyone, including Ritchie Thornton. Aaron told me you'd had more trouble than that. I want to explain everything to you first."

"That'd be nice," Fargo remarked.

Ruth Larkin's eyes told him she'd caught the reproof in the comment. "We're a group of small, independent ranchers. Aaron didn't lie about anything when he hired you to break a new trail for us," she said.

"He just didn't tell me the whole truth," Fargo said. "And that doesn't make me happy. It seems there's a whole lot more than just breaking a new trail to this."

"We didn't expect all this would happen. We certainly didn't expect they'd go after you," Ruth Larkin explained, and he heard the truth in her voice.

"Who's they?" he questioned.

"Howard Simmons and Blythe Donnen. They're the Cattlemen's Combine. Oh, Ed Sowerby's in with them too, but he's just tagalong and goes with whatever they say," the woman told him. "The combine owns all the flatland leading south from Mountainville. To drive our steers to Albuquerque we have to cross their land."

"They can't own the whole damn plains," Fargo said.

"They own all the land in a circle from the edge of the mountains out far enough so nobody can drive cattle south to New Mexico without crossing it," the woman answered.

"You see, they've been letting us drive across their

lands and charging us fifty cents a head," Aaron Highbard cut in. "That means we sometimes actually lost money when we sold in Albuquerque. Now they've raised it to a dollar a head. None of us can pay that. Cattle prices won't permit it. That's why we have to find a trail through the San Juan foothills."

"And that's why they've decided to do anything they can to stop us, and it seems that includes stopping you from finding a new trail for us," Ruth Larkin resumed. "You're right; it's not just breaking a new trail anymore. Without a new trail we're finished. They know it, of course." The woman paused, drew a deep breath, and her round, full breasts pressed the plain gray dress tight. "That's all of it, except for meeting everyone."

A hardworking middle-aged man with a strong face stepped forward, a youth about twenty or so years beside him and a small, wiry-framed woman alongside him. "Sam Dunstan, my boy, Lemuel, and my wife, Mary," the man said.

Another man moved up, a younger man with a young, open-faced woman beside him. "Dennis Toolan, my wife, Elsa," he said. "We've two hands that work for us when we drive our herd."

A big man with a black beard and the hands of a bear took a big-footed step forward. His dark eyes frowned at Fargo. "Armstrong," he snapped. "I'll tell you right off. I didn't agree we needed a trailsman. I figure I can find us a way, but I was outvoted."

"Always appreciate a man who speaks his mind," Fargo replied.

A black-haired, stern-faced man stepped forward next, and Richie Thornton followed him. Another youth, perhaps a year younger than Ritchie, appeared and hurried over.

"Ed Thornton, Ritchie and Henny. We're ready for

herdin' or fightin', whichever it has to be," the older man said belligerently.

Fargo nodded and turned to the last of those gathered before him, two men in their early thirties, square, strong faces with two equally determined-looking young women at their sides.

"Mike Hennessy, my wife, Sarah," the first one said. "My brother, Pat, and his missus, Grace." The two men moved back as Aaron Highbard came forward.

"There you have it, Fargo. All of us are small ranchers, and we don't hanker to be big cattlemen. We want just enough steers to make a comfortable living," Aaron said.

Fargo surveyed the group, counting silently as he did. Seventeen in all, including wives and young boys. "You pool men and steers when you drive?" he asked.

"We have up to now, with Sam Dunstan's two hired hands thrown in and a few others if we can afford them," Aaron answered. "Sometimes, the womenfolk go along, too."

Fargo's eyes fastened on Ruth Larkin as the woman spoke up. "I guess Aaron should have told you all of it right from the start," she said.

"That's how I see it," Fargo agreed coldly.

"I'll take the blame for that," Ruth Larkin said, holding his gaze steadily. "I thought it'd be simpler not to go into all the details then."

"Maybe you're still holding back a few things," Fargo commented.

"No," Ruth Larkin said sharply, and he shrugged as her eyes searched his face. "You saying you're not going to break trail for us now?" she asked.

"I'm saying I'm going to think on it some more," Fargo answered. "That'll give you time to remember anything else you might be forgetting to mention."

"There isn't anything else," the woman said.

"Then it'll give me time to do some checking around for myself," Fargo said.

"You've a right," Ruth Larkin said. "Seeing as how we did hold back. But we need you. We need to find a new trail to drive out steers down to Albuquerque."

"Guess you'll let Ruth know what you decide," Aaron Highbard said, and Fargo nodded.

"My place is the other side of town, big red cedar in front," Ruth Larkin said.

"I'll find it," Fargo said, nodded to the others as he swung into the saddle. They watched him ride off, their silence one of disappointment and apprehension. It didn't bother him any as he cantered back toward town. They hadn't said anything about a pretty blond night rider helping their cause. Did that mean something? he asked himself. Were they still holding something back? The question rode with him as he turned the pinto and made a wide circle around town and rode to the edge of the mountains where the foothills rose sharply. He halted beneath a bur oak, dismounted, and let his gaze sweep the lower reaches of the San Juan range. He felt his lips draw back in a grimace. It was sure as hell no terrain for driving cattle. Maybe he could find a trail through the lower range. Maybe, he grunted. But even if he did, there was the Cheyenne. The plains were too vast to stop all the white man's covered wagons and cattle drives. But the mountain strongholds were a different matter. The Cheyenne wouldn't permit that kind of invasion, and Fargo turned away with his lips drawn thin.

He sat down and waited until the night began to roll across the land like a vast black blanket unfolding. He rose as a new moon appeared in the sky, took a fresh shirt from his saddlebags, and changed into it. He rode north when he'd finished, onto the flatland, and the Simmons ranch came into sight, a big, impressive main house blazing with light and long corrals spreading out on both sides. Two men with rifles watched him from the front yard as he rode to a halt. He scanned the rigs that circled the front of the big house, saw a few buckboards but more fancy landaus, gentlemen's driving phaetons, surreys, and a round-bottomed brett. He crossed to the open front door of the house, heard the murmur of men's and women's voices as he entered.

His eyes swept a large room, handsomely furnished with oak furniture that had been cleared to one side. The walls were decorated with oil paintings of nature scenes, and thick, deep-red drapes covered the windows. It was a room that spoke of wealth and comfort. Women in fancy ball gowns and men mostly in dress clothes filled the room, some dancing to a piano player in one corner. He watched Howard Simmons come to meet him, a small man at his side. Simmons wore a ruffled shirt and a black velvet jacket, the other man more modestly dressed.

"Glad you made it, Fargo," Howard Simmons greeted. "This is one of my associates, Ed Sowerby."

Fargo took the hand Ed Sowerby extended and thought of how Ruth Larkin had characterized the man. Perhaps she was right, but Fargo saw crafty, quick-appraising eyes in an otherwise bland, slightly puffy face. "All of these good folks your associates?" Fargo asked Simmons with a nod toward the crowd.

"Hell, no." Simmons laughed. "I give a party every month, and most of these folks are just old friends, many of them don't live anywhere near here. There are a few cattle buyers and county officials. And there is someone I want you to meet. Meanwhile, go get yourself a drink."

"Much obliged," Fargo said, and strolled to where a white-jacketed man served drinks from a wooden

42

cart. Fargo took a bourbon and elbowed his way through the merrymakers. He exchanged small talk with a woman wearing too much jewelry, and a few older men. One, a silvery-haired man with sharp blue eyes introduced himself as the chief clerk of the land survey office. "Thomas Boyard," he said, and shook hands vigorously.

A woman stopped, her eyes taking in the chiseled handsomeness of the big man with the lake-blue eyes. "My, Howard is inviting handsomer men these days," she murmured. "You're a newcomer to these affairs."

"Just stopping by. Name's Skye Fargo," the Trailsman said.

"Well, I do hope you'll find a reason to stay around," the woman said, and swept on with a grand gesture.

Fargo moved on through the crowd as he sipped his bourbon and admired the paintings that covered the walls. He had just skirted around a knot of earnest conversationalists when he all but colllided with the young woman that hurried from an adjoining room.

He halted and saw her face mirror the astonishment that flooded through him as her nicely modeled lips dropped open. Her blond hair hung loose now, down to her shoulders, and she wore a pink dress with a square neck that hinted at high, firm breasts. But there was no mistaking her, and for the first time he could see her eyes. They were the soft gray of a mockingbird's breasts. They were exchanging stares, and she found her voice first. "What are you doing here?" she hissed.

"I was invited. What the hell are you doing here?" he tossed back.

"I live here," she snapped, and he felt the frown dig into his brow.

"You and I are going to do some talking," Fargo said.

"Not here," she whispered fiercely, and he saw her eyes go past him and her face grow composed. He glanced back to see Howard Simmons walking toward him.

"I see you've met my daughter." The man smiled, and Fargo managed to keep another flood of surprise out of his face. But when Howard Simmons halted beside her, the even features bore out the resemblance at once.

"I think she was wondering if I crashed your party," Fargo said smoothly.

"Oh, no." The man laughed, and tossed a glance at his daughter. "This is Skye Fargo, the Trailsman. The independents have asked him to find a new trail for them."

The girl allowed a quick smile. "I'm Avery," she said, and Fargo saw her mask the nervousness that nonetheless edged the corners of her lips. "Nice to meet you," she said, and hurried away, the long blond hair swinging from side to side.

"Come into the study," Howard Simmons said, and led the way into a wood-paneled room with sturdy chairs, an oak table, and a black leather sofa. A woman there turned, and Fargo saw sharp blue eyes take him in from head to toe with one sweeping glance. He also saw an exceedingly handsome woman, perhaps thirty or so, he guessed. Very white skin and very black hair made a striking contrast while a straight nose and full red lips completed a face that seemed to vibrate sensuality. A tight bright-green dress outlined longish breasts, a narrow waist, and nicely curved thighs.

"My associate, Blythe Donnen," Simmons introduced, and Fargo let one eyebrow lift in surprise.

"My pleasure, Fargo," the woman said, a huskiness in her voice that only added to the sensuality of her. "Howard said you were attractive. He understated the truth of it," she said.

"Well, you're the best-looking damn cattleman I ever saw." Fargo grinned.

"I must get back to my guests, Fargo," Simmons cut in. "Blythe will speak for all of us. She's not only the beauty but the brains behind the combine." He leaned over, kissed Blythe Donnen on the cheek, let his hand linger for a moment along the small of her back, the gesture more than casual. Fargo watched the woman give Simmons a private little smile, and the man hurried from the room.

"The brains as well as the beauty," Fargo echoed. "Does that mean you're the one who had me set up back in Ten Rocks?"

Her smile was slow. "I like a man who's direct," she said.

"Direct saves time," Fargo remarked.

"No, it doesn't mean that." Blythe Donnen laughed, a low delicious sound. "We're not the only ones who don't want the independents finding new trails. There's a big rancher in New Mexico, Arguilla by name. He doesn't want them bringing their steers down to Albuquerque at all. He's wealthy, ruthless, and it'd be his style to go after you. They told plenty of people they were hiring you."

"I'll keep that in mind," Fargo said. "It seems your style is to own one hell of a lot of land."

"No law against that," the woman replied.

"It seems as though it was staked out to do just what you're doing," Fargo said. Blythe Donnen dismissed the comment with a shrug. "There's a thing called passage rights," he pressed.

"We don't deny ordinary passage rights. People

ride across it all the time—wagon trains, too. We're willing to let the independents drive through," Blythe Donnen said.

"At a price they can't afford," Fargo said.

"That's their problem. They run their operations right, they could pay, but they want to stay small," she answered.

"They've a right to do that," he said.

"And we've a right to charge them. The land's ours, claimed and deeded," she said. "But we want to make you an offer. The Cheyenne have been getting bolder in their raids. We want you to take our next drive through, find a trail not so open or so damn hot. We'll pay you twice whatever they've offered."

"I've been hired," he said.

"Forget that. They're not worth helping, Fargo. They're small time, nothing, land grubbers. The cattle market will be better off without them," the woman said.

"I don't break my word," Fargo told her.

Blythe Donnen's slow smile was made of many things, and confidence was one of them. "I appreciate that, but you should think again on this one. I'd like to try to convince you to make an exception," she said, letting the unsaid words hang heavily in the air.

"Never stop a lady from trying," Fargo said.

"Good." Blythe Donnen smiled. "Strictly between us, of course. Howard is really quite straightlaced."

Fargo held thoughts inside himself as he slid out one more question. "What if I decide to keep my word and find them a trail?" he asked.

She shrugged. "I won't be happy, but that's life," she said.

"The rest of your people going to take it so lightly," he questioned.

"Of course, but you'd best think about Arguilla. He reaches far out."

Fargo caught a flash of pink in the doorway and saw Avery Simmons there. "Howard in here?" she asked, but Fargo noted her eyes were on himself and Blythe Donnen.

"No, dear," Blythe said, and her tone was suddenly sweet coldness.

Avery Simmons disappeared from the doorway. "Pretty gal, that one," he commented.

"Isn't she?" the woman agreed, but her tone was one of pure dismissal.

"I'll be going on now," Fargo said. "Thanks for the offer."

"I'm told you're the very best. You agree with that, I presume," Blythe Donnen said, a little smile of toying amusement touching her full, red lips.

"If you're talking about trailing, riding, shooting, drinking, and screwing, I agree," he said blandly. "I'll be in touch."

He walked from the room, and her low, sensuous chuckle followed after him. He glanced about for Avery Simmons, trying to find a flash of pink in the crowd as he crossed the main room, but there was none. Howard Simmons saw him as he reached the door and waved. Fargo went on outside, unhitched the Ovaro, and rode slowly away from the ranch. The two men with their rifles were still in the front yard, he noted.

He rode slowly under the new moon, and when he decided he'd gone far enough, he turned and doubled back in a wide circle that brought him to a thin line of cottonwoods. He pulled the pinto close to the trees, followed along the edge of the thin trunks until the ranch came into sight. The trees marched almost to the back of the house. When he drew closer, he halted and dismounted, leaving the horse and continuing on foot to where he could clearly see the main house. He dropped down to the grass, leaned back against a tree trunk, and relaxed. The party was still going strong. He'd have plenty of time to wait and digest what he had learned.

Surprises never stopped, it seemed, and Fargo decided to start with Blythe Donnen. Simmons had been right about one thing: she was more than beauty. She was smart. But whether she really ran the cattlemen's combine remained unanswered. He remembered the craftiness of Ed Sowerby's eyes. As for Simmons, it had quickly become plain that he had more than a business relationship with Blythe Donnen. Or, at least, he wanted more. She might well be keeping him dangling, Fargo mused. She'd be the type, he grunted.

Blythe Donnen's offer had been pretty damn transparent, little more than an attempt to keep him from helping the independents. But her efforts to convince him might be worth the trip. He smiled. He sure intended to find out. But his eyes grew narrow as he thought about the rest of her denials. She hadn't manufactured the New Mexico rancher. That would be too easy to check out, and she was too smart for that. There undoubtedly was a Señor Arguilla, but she could have dragged him in as a fast answer to his question. It was all still wrapped in the unanswered. Half-truths seemed to be an all-around habit here, and his thoughts turned to a very pretty little blond package. She had a name now, and was even more of an enigma. Avery Simmons was playing some kind of game, maybe a very dangerous one. But what? And why?

The questions were left hanging as he heard the murmur of voices and sat up straight to watch two couples leave the house and hurry into a wine-colored landau. Others followed, and he saw Blythe Donnen come out alone and climb into a buckboard. The affair was ending. Fargo rose to one knee, his gaze fixed on the front of the house as others strolled out. He saw Ed Sowerby leave, mount a dark bay, and ride off. Still others were coming out, and Fargo saw Howard Simmons come to the door to bid his guests good night. A pink dress became a flash of brightness as Avery came to stand beside him.

Fargo stayed motionless on one knee, watched until the last guest left and Simmons went into the house with his daughter, closing the door behind him. Fargo saw the two men with the rifles leave the front yard and walk back toward the corrals before disappearing into the darkness.

As the lights in the house went out one by one, Fargo scanned the windows until he saw the second-floor window suddenly light. He caught a glimpse of pink for an instant and marked the window in his mind. A few moments later, the light went out. He waited, making certain the house had grown completely still and dark before he moved from the thin row of trees. He ran in a crouch, long legs carrying him to the back of the house where he dropped to one knee beneath a partly opened window. He rose, grasped the window with both hands, and lifted. When he had it opened wide enough, he pulled himself in over the sill and dropped to the floor inside. He immediately smelled the wood and leather and knew he was in the study. A small lamp in the hallway afforded just enough dim light for him to make his way across the room to the open doorway and find the steps that led to the second floor.

He moved on silent steps along the second-floor hall to the closed door of the room he'd marked in his mind. He closed one big hand around the doorknob, slowly eased the door open, and closed it behind him with equal silence. A large bed almost touched the edge of the window, the cascade of blond hair covering the pillow. He crossed the room in three long, silent strides, halted alongside the bed, and peered down at the sleeping figure. Avery Simmons wore a silk nightgown as she lay on her side, and he let himself enjoy the round, full edge of her right breast, which spilled half out of the nightgown. He reached out, pressed his hand gently but firmly over her mouth, and her eyes snapped open at once. She half-turned, stared up at him as he kept his hand over her mouth.

"Quiet," he growled.

Her eyes were round as gray saucers as she stared at him over the edge of his hand. She nodded and he drew his hand away. She sat up instantly. "Are you mad?" she hissed.

"I want some answers from you, honey," Fargo said.

She swung from the bed, and he saw full, round breasts bounce. She pulled on a silk robe from a chair and wriggled into it. "Get out of here before somebody finds you," she whispered hoarsely.

"Not until you explain a few things," Fargo said.

"Not now. Not here," Avery Simmons hissed again. "My father's in the next room. He's a very light sleeper. He'll hear us and there are guards downstairs."

"I didn't see any guards," Fargo said.

"You were lucky, dammit. Get out of here before your luck runs out," she insisted.

"Not without some answers," he said.

"Tomorrow. I'll meet you tomorrow," she said, and

he heard the note of desperation in her whispered urgency. "Please, go. I can't talk here. I won't."

He studied her for a moment. "Where?" he asked.

"There's a lake, straight north through the first steep pass in the hills. Tomorrow midmorning," she whispered.

He heard a man's cough from the next room and saw the panic leap into her eyes. "Tomorrow morning," he grunted, crossed the room in three long strides, and eased the door open again.

"Be careful downstairs," he heard her whisper as he closed the door silently behind him and slipped into the dim hallway.

He crept down the steps to the floor below and had just reached the doorway of the study when he saw the figure round the corner at the far end of the hall. He disappeared into the study, swung himself out of the window, and ran to the row of trees in a low crouch. She hadn't lied about the guards, he conceded grimly as he hurried through the trees to the Ovaro. He took the horse through the trees at a walk, increased his speed only when he had cleared the other edge of the trees, and headed south until he found a spot to bed down for the night. He had things planned before he'd meet with Avery in the morning.

4

Fargo slept soundly and woke with the sun, dressed, found some wild plums for breakfast, and rode back in the general direction of the Simmons ranch. But he made a wide circle before he neared it and headed slowly out onto the plains. His eyes narrowed in thought as they swept the flatland to where the foothills of the San Juan range rose. He spotted four horsemen riding easily across the deep grass and turned the Ovaro to cut across their path. They halted as he came up, four cowhands on sturdy herding ponies, leather chaps worn smooth from hard riding.

" 'Morning," Fargo called out. "You from around here?" One of the men nodded. "I'm looking for the Donnen spread," Fargo said.

"That way," the cowhand said, and pointed north. "You'll see it, big spread, well-kept."

Fargo let his eyes move out across the flatland. "All this combine land?" he asked casually, and the man nodded. "How far does it go?" Fargo queried.

"Far as you can see, mister," the cowhand said. "We ought to know. We work for Howard Simmons."

Fargo let himself look impressed. It wasn't hard to do

as he swept the wide expanse of land again with a glance. "Mighty impressive," he intoned. "Much obliged," he added as he turned the pinto west.

Simmons' men spurred their horses forward, and Fargo rode slowly west until they were well on their way. He turned then and headed north, his lips drawn in tight as he scanned the horizon line again. Too much, he muttered to himself. Too damn much land. Something wasn't right. He couldn't see the territory land office allowing claims to that much prairie land, not just to three ranchers acting as a combine. It just didn't set right. Yet Blythe Donnen had said the land was claimed and deeded. He was still frowning when he reached the foothills and found the first steep path.

He rode upward through a border of flat-walled shale that ended abruptly, and he suddenly found himself in front of an almost perfectly round lake—a beautiful spot nestled in a hollow. White birch and box elder grew almost to the water's edge, and he made his way along the narrow space along the shore, ducking his head to avoid low-hanging branches. The lake was a lot deeper into the foothills than he'd expected, and he scanned the thick trees that covered the surrounding hills, his gaze lingering at each break in the trees. But he saw nothing unwelcome, and he dismounted. He settled himself on the grassy bank and leaned back on his elbows, relaxing as he waited, trailing his fingers in the water as he watched the sun dance with little sparkling steps across the lake. The bird songs filled the stillness, goldfinch and orioles, wood thrush and waxwings.

The sun grew hot, he shed jacket and shirt, and the cool water beckoned. He rose, walked farther along the bank to where a white birch leaned over the water. He shed the rest of his clothes, hung his gun belt at the end of the lowest branch where he could easily reach it, and slipped into the lake. The water slid around his hard-packed frame, cooling, refreshing, delightfully welcome as the sun moved higher. He dived beneath the surface, came up again, and paused to sweep the shoreline with a glance. Nothing moved, and he turned on his back and let himself float lazily. He squinted up at the sun and felt a stab of irritation. She was late. Midmorning had come and gone. He continued to float, broke the time with quick dives beneath the surface, and the sun continued to move across the cloudless sky. The irritation inside him began to turn to apprehension and then to anger.

She wasn't coming, he finally concluded angrily. It was past noon, dammit, he swore. She wasn't coming, probably never intended to come. Goddamn, he bit out again. She'd tossed him a fast promise to get rid of him, and he'd believed her. She'd saved his neck, but she wouldn't come to meet him. It didn't make any damn sense. She didn't make any sense.

Fargo turned to the shore, started to stand up in the water when he saw the branches move a dozen yards down the bank. He sank down instantly, only his eyes and the top of his head above the water as he watched the trees. He searched for a flash of blond hair, but there was none. Instead, he caught the glint of sunlight glisten on very black hair as Blythe Donnen came into sight on a dapple-gray standardbred.

He saw her spot the Ovaro at once, and her eyes went to the lake. He rose, stood up in the water again, and saw Blythe Donnen focus on him, her eyes taking in the glistening beauty of his muscled frame. He stayed in place, the surface of the water just below his hips, and Blythe Donnen moved the dapple-gray slowly toward him along the bank. She wore a black shirt that emphasized the whiteness of her skin and matched the blackness of her hair. "You do get around, Fargo," she said with a little smile, quiet amusement in her husky voice.

"Happened to be out riding and came onto it," Fargo said. "Couldn't resist having a dip."

"It is a lovely spot, hidden away. I often come here to do just what you're doing," Blythe Donnen said.

"Alone?" he asked, his brows lifting. "You could have Cheyenne for company up this far."

"Two of my men stay at the mouth of the pass. I scream, and they'll come running," the woman said. She dismounted and walked to the edge of the water.

"The lake's all yours. I was just leaving," Fargo said.

"Do you want me to turn my back," Blythe said, the amusement still in her voice.

"Do you want to?" he answered.

"No," she said.

He shrugged and stepped from the water as her eyes devoured him. "Magnificent," she whispered as he sank down on the grass to let the sun dry him. He felt his loins stirring at her presence. Her fingers began to unbutton the shirt, and he saw the white curve of her longish breasts.

"You want me to turn my back?" he asked.

"Do you want to?" she returned.

"No," he said.

She laughed and slipped the blouse off, letting it fall to the grass. The long breasts were very white and they filled out at the bottoms, curved upward beautifully, each alabaster mound centered with a deep-pink circle and a brown-pink nipple. The woman leaned over, slipped off white bloomers, and paused for a moment at the water's edge to let him take in the long, full thighs that curved down from wide hips, a small, rounded belly, and beneath it, a dense, wiry triangle that seemed even blacker than it was against the very white skin.

"Nice, real nice," Fargo murmured as she stepped into the lake and walked slowly deeper into the water. Her breasts swayed in unison as she walked, beautifully provocative. Blythe Donnen finally sank into the water, turned on her back, and floated for a moment, breasts surfacing just enough to let the brown-pink tips thrust upward. She turned, swam, dived, surfaced, and rose half out of the water. She shook the glistening black hair, stretched, and her breasts lifted, shining with wetness.

"Hell," Fargo muttered, rose, and started to step into the water.

"No," she said sharply. "Not here."

He halted, slid a slow smile at her. "Be real nice here," he said.

"No," she said, an unexpected plea in her tone. "Tonight, at my place. I'll expect you. Tonight, please."

He shrugged, reached for his trousers. "I'll be going then," he said, and she nodded, her eyes watching his gravely. To stay and watch her would be too damn frustrating, he grumbled to himself, as he dressed quickly and swung onto the Ovaro.

She waved as he rode away, standing half out of the water, long breasts glistening. He frowned as he pushed through the trees. She had deliberately tantalized him, and then suddenly came her refusal, sharp, adamant, almost fearful. But he'd be taking up her invitation for sure.

He passed the two men at the mouth of the pass, one hard-faced with a scarred upper lip, the other a weasely type with stringy hair. Fargo rode on, and the sun was in the midafternoon sky when he reached the base of the foothills. Anger settled down over him again as his thoughts returned to Avery Simmons. She wasn't going to get away with it, he muttered grimly. He was going to find out what kind of game she was playing. But that would have to wait till tomorrow. The Simmons ranch was too open to just go barging in. He turned the Ovaro toward Mountainville and circled past on the other side of town. He spied the red cedar in front of Ruth Larkin's place, saw a barn bigger than the ranch house and some twenty longhorns in a corral attached to the barn.

Ruth Larkin had company, he saw as he rode up to the house. Aaron Highbard and Dennis Toolan sat in a buckboard, and Armstrong's big, burly frame was settled on a heavy-legged brown horse. Ruth Larkin stepped forward as Fargo dismounted. "We were just talking about you, Fargo," the woman said, her direct, brown eyes searching his face. "Did you come to give us your decision?"

"No," Fargo said. "I came to find out if there was anything more you'd forgotten to tell me about."

"There isn't anything more. How long are you going to keep thinking we're holding back?" Ruth Larkin said sharply.

"Till I'm sure you're not," Fargo said calmly.

"I don't give a damn what you think, Fargo," Armstrong broke in. "I just told Ruth and Aaron I don't trust anyone who goes to Howard Simmons' fancy parties."

"News gets around." Fargo smiled.

"Some of Simmons' hands laughed at me in town, said that the trailsman we hired had sold out already," Armstrong barked.

"Is that true, Fargo?" Ruth Larkin asked, anxiousness and apprehension in her voice.

"It's true about my being at the party." Fargo half-laughed. "Simmons asked me to come. I thought it'd be a good chance to look, listen, and learn for myself. If I'm going to lock horns with someone, I want to know as much as I can about him. That's not selling out. That's good sense."

"So it is," Aaron Highbard agreed.

"Fargo's not the selling-out kind, not from what I've heard," Ruth Larkin said to Armstrong. "He may turn us down, but I don't believe he'd sell us out."

"Couldn't have said it better myself," Fargo smiled.

"What'd you find out at Simmons' place?" she asked.

"Not enough yet," Fargo admitted. "But I figure to keep looking around."

"There's nothing to find out. They've got the land, they want to squeeze us to death, and we've got to get a trail through the mountains," Armstrong said angrily.

"Maybe it's not all that simple," Fargo said. "I'm going up into the mountains on my own and scout around some. I'll tell you what I find, and you can decide from there."

"That sounds fair enough to me," Aaron said, and Ruth Larkin nodded agreement.

Armstrong only scowled. "You go ahead with him. I'll stand by what I said," he barked, and sent his horse into a fast trot.

"He's always been a hard-nosed man," Aaron Highbard said. "But he's a hard worker."

"A man has his own ways, right or wrong," Fargo remarked, and climbed onto the pinto.

Ruth Larkin stepped to stand beside the horse, her brown, direct eyes peering steadily up at him. "Come by whenever you want," she said. "Whether you're ready for deciding or not."

He nodded and wondered if he detected a very

female stirring under that no-nonsense, sturdy, quiet exterior. Suddenly he sensed something, but he pushed aside the stray thought and took the pinto away at a fast canter. He headed west under the growing moon, found the place where the two roads crossed, and took the top one until he reached a large spread—long corrals, a fair-sized main house, and two big barns. He rode in and slowed as he neared the main house, where two outdoor lamps lighted the front yard. A cowhand crossed in front of him carrying a saddle toward a bunkhouse, and he saw it was the scar-lipped man. Fargo tied the pinto to a hitching post and started for the front door of the house. He had just about reached it when the door swung open.

"Welcome," Blythe Donnen said, her low, husky voice giving the word a special flavor that her slow smile echoed. She wore a floor-length, form-fitting white gown that made her gleaming black hair and black eyebrows look almost painted. A row of buttons went down the entire length of the front of the gown, and the garment followed the contours of her body with every step. She closed the door behind him, and he followed her into a luxurious living room with two thick, dark-brown sofas and a pair of bearskin rugs. She gestured to a tray on a round table. "Roast beef and bourbon," she said. "I thought you might be hungry."

"I am, but I was thinking of nibbling on something else first," Fargo remarked.

The slow smile grew a fraction wider as she turned and began to walk from the room, her rear moving sinuously under the tightness of the gown. He followed her down a corridor and into a bedroom where a double bed, the headstand painted white, took up most of the room. Pillows in various colors were casually strewn about, and Blythe Donnen halted, turned to him, and nodded to the door. He closed it and she began to unbutton the top buttons of the long satin garment. Her long, alabaster breasts pushed out into plain view when she reached the middle buttons and she continued to unbutton the gown with deliberate, tantalizing slowness. The long, smooth waist came into sight, then the rounded little belly, and she halted, wriggled her shoulders and hips, and the gown fluttered to the floor.

The tall, sensuous beauty he'd seen at the lake was no less so now, and he felt himself responding to her at once as he shed clothes. He was growing, rising even before he'd taken off the last piece of his clothes. He saw Blythe Donnen's eyes on him, a dark, turbulent flame setting the blue pupils afire. She took a step toward him, her eyes fastened on his now throbbing, pulsating organ. She came against him, and his maleness thrust itself between her thighs. She almost fell backward, her hands closing around his neck as she pulled him onto the bed with her. His mouth found the pink-brown tip of one breast and pulled, took the soft little nipple into his mouth, and Blythe Donnen groaned with a combination of unbearable pleasure and unrestrained wanting.

He sank his face onto the long, alabaster mounds, and she groaned again. No short, gasped cries, but wild, passionate groans filled with longing. Blythe Donnen cried out as he caressed, sucked, pulled. He felt her long legs lifting, falling open, and her hands were pounding against his chest, his shoulders, and he swung his body over hers, pressed his warm, wanting organ down onto the pure white skin and again she cried out with desire. She half-rose, drew back, lifted the dense black tangle, and he let his organ fall through the wiry brush. Her cries began to mingle with one another, becoming a wild, wailing sound with each caress of her breasts, with each touch of his maleness against her. He lifted, brought his throbbing warmth to the flowing portal, and plunged in, and Blythe Donnen's voice rose, stayed, hung in the air.

He pushed into her and her groans matched his thrusts, rose with each, reached new heights. Her alabaster breasts shook violently as she quivered and quaked with her entire body. "Now, Fargo," Blythe Donnen demanded, and her cries hurtled from her as she came, her dark, moist tunnel of softness trembling, pushing around him, clinging to him with each instant, spasmodic contraction. Her voice had grown hoarse and breathy. He stayed inside her as she went limp, and he saw the black hair against the white bedcover grow still as she lay as if unconscious, her eyes closed, her body still.

He drew from her slowly, and she gave a protesting sound, but her eyes remained closed. He sank down beside her, his face into the round, full bottom of a long, alabaster breast. He drew a deep breath, as much of surprise as of exhaustion. It was plain now why she had refused so adamantly at the lake. Half the San Juan range would have heard her, to say nothing of her two hands at the pass. He watched as her eyes slowly came open and focused on him.

"God, Fargo," she said breathlessly as she pushed herself up on one elobw. Her eyes still were half-closed as she fell against him, pushed her face across his chest, down over his abdomen. She pressed her mouth into his skin as he felt her fingers moving down his body, through the wire-soft nap of hair, and close around his still-half-rigid maleness.

She held him and made little wailing sounds. He

felt himself answering to her touch at once, and he heard her gasped intake of breath. She fell onto her back as she pulled him with her, pushing her long legs open and bringing him to her.

"Again, oh God, again," Blythe Donnen said, the huskiness of her voice rising to a strident plea. He felt her soft, moist lips surrounding him, and he slid forward into her. Her cry was instant and intense, and once again her cries continued to surprise him with their unending power until finally there was only one, long cry as she climaxed and fell limply back onto the bed with him.

He lay beside her, his gaze moving over the very white, almost chalklike color of her smooth skin, the long breasts that grew into beautifully molded shapes.

She opened her eyes slowly, took a moment to focus on him, and the slow smile of contained amusement touched her lips. "Surprised?" she murmured, her voice low and husky once more.

"Some," he admitted. "You holler up a storm."

She half-shrugged and the two alabaster mounds swayed in unison. "It's always been that way with me. Maybe it keeps me from becoming too loose. I have to be careful." She laughed.

"I'm hungry," Fargo said, swung from the bed, and went into the living room to return with the tray of beef slices and the bourbon.

Blythe Donnen sat cross-legged atop the bed as she ate, the long breasts dipping and moving together and all enveloped in simmering sensuality. But the cool, contained, toying amusement was in hand once again as she regarded him with both appreciation and conjecture. She leaned forward when they'd finished eating, and he set the tray on a small night table. "This could be a regular thing," she murmured.

"If I stayed and found you a new trail," he finished.

"That's right," she said, her face only inches from his.

"What happens to Simmons?" Fargo asked casually. "I got the impression he's more than just a business partner."

She leaned back a little. "I can handle Howard, just as I do now. If he becomes a nuisance, I'll find another partner. You, maybe," she said. She came forward again, slid arms around his neck, and rubbed the long breasts back and forth across his chest. "Are you becoming convinced?" she murmured into his ear.

"You're sure as hell getting an A for effort," Fargo said.

Blythe Donnen drew back, her eyes narrowed as she studied him. The slow smile came again to touch her lips. "I want more than that, Fargo," she said. She had a way of letting the little sensuous smile veil an edge of thinness in her tone, he noted.

"I need a little more time," he said mildly.

She thought for a moment. "Everyone has to break their word once in a while," she said.

"Do it once, and it becomes right easy, doesn't it?" Fargo smiled.

Blythe reached for her gown without comment, began to slip it on, and he rose and dressed, aware that her eyes stayed on the muscled beauty of his body until he was clothed. She walked to the door with him, her hips rubbing against his leg. Her sharp blue eyes were darkened as she turned to him. "Principles are a luxury, Fargo. And there are more enjoyable luxuries," she said.

"There sure are," he said, and let his hand rub across the twin mounds of her soft rear as he pulled the door open.

"When will you be stopping by again?" she asked.

"Soon as I need some more convincing," he said, and walked into the darkness.

"Don't wait too long," Blythe called after him, the words both an appeal and a warning.

He took the pinto and rode slowly from the ranch, crossed the flat prairie land, and turned north to where he found a pair of cottonwoods that made a good place to bed down. He unsaddled the pinto, took out his bedroll, and undressed. Stretched out in the night, he let his thoughts unwind. The conflict seemed simple enough on the surface—the need for the small independent ranchers to find a new trail or be squeezed out of existence. Only there was something else. He felt it inside himself. It was more than just big against little, greed against survival. Somebody was too bothered for just that. They'd tried to kill him back at Ten Rocks. All to stop him from finding a new trail? Or to make sure he didn't find something more?

His thoughts held on Blythe Donnen. In a way she was a reflection of everything else about this place. She had been more than he'd expected, and he could still hear her cries of pure pleasure. But he found himself wondering if perhaps that wasn't the only uncalculated part of her. She had invited him with more than bed in mind. Blythe Donnen was able to let her needs and her wants dovetail, balling and bargaining, passion and purpose. Then there was a distant presence named Arguilla and a little blond night rider who seemed bent on helping her father's opponents.

It was all like a picture where everything was slightly distorted. It appeared ordinary at first glance but nothing was really right, and Fargo was growing more and more certain that a mysterious little blond night rider could furnish the answers. He turned on his side, closed his eyes, and slept, plans already formed in his mind.

5

The tall man with the lake-blue eyes sat motionless in the saddle as the dawn edged its way across the sky. There wasn't enough real cover to hide in broad daylight near the Simmons ranch, so he'd settled for a pair of low shadbush on a distant hillock. The ranch appeared a collection of toy buildings, the figures beginning to move about only tiny forms. But he kept his eyes straining as he sought only a flash of blond hair. Sometime, Avery Simmons would ride out, he felt certain, and he'd wait for that moment.

The wait was shorter than he'd expected, and the sun was climbing over the mountain peaks when he saw the lone rider emerge from one of the buildings and ride north. He caught the glint of blond hair under a flat-brimmed hat and watched the horse covering ground in a fast trot. He wheeled the Ovaro off to the side as he began to follow. He paralleled her path, but stayed far enough away to make certain she didn't pick him up. When she continued on into the low hills with plenty of tree cover, he speeded the pinto on into the trees and picked up her trail of bent branches and turned leaves.

She was threading her way up the low hills through

thick underbrush and heavy growths of staghorn sumac and buckthorn, climbing steadily until the terrain leveled off in a series of rolling hills. As he followed, Fargo kept one eye on the surrounding terrain, alert for the sudden flash of copper-hued bodies. But the thick lush foliage revealed only various shades of green, and Fargo moved the Ovaro closer as he followed Avery Simmons' path. Though he still stayed back, he drew close enough to glimpse her as she rode through the brush. He moved closer as she sent the roan out of the brush and trees and into a small, cleared hollow. He followed her and saw a one-room, tumbledown shack with one window and sagging walls.

He halted in the trees and watched her dismount and stride into the cabin. She wore a yellow, tailored blouse over her black riding skirt, he saw. He waited until she emerged from the shack, and his eyes widened as he saw her leading a slender, bald-headed man by the hand. Fargo edged the pinto closer to the little hollow as Avery Simmons brought the man to a tree stump and sat him down on it as though he were a child.

"You stay right there, Abel. I brought your favorite biscuits," she said, and Fargo watched as she went to her saddlebag and brought out biscuits and beef slices wrapped in paper.

He brought the Ovaro to the edge of the hollow, swung to the ground. He was now close enough to see the man clearly, a lined face under the bald pate that wore a childlike, half-vacant expression. As he watched, a frown digging into his brow, Avery Simmons began to hand-feed the man pieces of the biscuit and the beef slices.

"That's good, Abel, you eat everything," she said, and the man nodded, his sudden smile adding to the childlike expression on his lined face. "It'll help make you strong so you can remember," Avery said.

"Yes, so I'll remember," the man repeated, and widened his vacant smile as he continued to eat with childlike gestures. When he finished, Avery cleaned up after him and returned to sit on the stump beside him.

"It's time to try again, Abel," she said. Abel smiled and nodded. "You were going away, remember?" Avery said.

"Yes, I was going away," Abel said, and smiled at her.

"They stopped you," Avery said.

"They stopped me," the man said, and began to frown.

"They hurt you. They tried to kill you," Avery prodded.

Abel's frown deepened as he stared into space. "Yes, I remember," he said.

"Now, think hard, Abel. Why did they try to kill you?" the girl asked, her tone soothing yet firm.

"They hurt me." The man frowned.

"Yes, they hurt you. But why, Abel?" Avery pressed. "Think hard. Remember."

Abel frowned so hard his bald head seemed to wrinkle, Fargo saw as he watched with fascination. "Can't . . . can't remember," the man muttered, and Fargo saw little beads of perspiration suddenly coating the bald head.

Avery's voice was soothing, calming as she patted his arm and used a kerchief to dry his forehead. "That's all right, Abel. Easy, now . . . easy. Just try to think," she murmured.

"They didn't—they didn't want me to go away," Abel said with a real effort.

"Very good, Abel, very good," the girl said in

praise, and Fargo caught the moment of excitement in her voice, "Why didn't they want you to go away, Abel? Think back, think hard."

Abel continued to frown into space. "Can't—can't remember," he said, and Fargo saw him begin to quiver.

Avery stood up, put her hands on his shoulders. "All right, all right, Abel. You're doing just fine. Easy, now . . . easy," she murmured. She sat down beside the man again as he stopped quivering, and Fargo saw her pat his arm. "Very good, Abel. You're doing very well," she said, and Abel's frown disappeared as he smiled at her the way a three-year-old smiles for approval. "Abel will remember more next time," Avery said. "Each time a little more."

The man nodded happily but his eyes still held their childlike gaze.

Fargo's eyes left Avery Simmons and the man suddenly as he caught the movement in the foliage at the edge of the back part of the hollow. The nearly naked, bronzed form stepped into view, moving on quick, silent footsteps. Cheyenne, by the markings on his browband, Fargo swore silently, tall, lithe, long-muscled, every movement catlike. Her attention completely on Abel, Avery was unaware of the Indian's presence until he seized her from behind. She gave a short scream as he flung her to the ground. Fargo saw Abel run with frightened, cowed motions, dart inside the shack as Avery reached into the waistband of her skirt. She tried to draw out the gun tucked there, but the Cheyenne saw it and lashed out with a kick that sent the six-gun flying from the girl's hand and doubled her up in pain at the same time.

The buck pounced on her at once, landing astride her as if he'd leapt onto a pony's back. Fargo saw a glimpse of nice, tanned calves as Avery's legs kicked out futilely, and he stepped from the trees, crossed the little hollow in a half-dozen swift strides. But the Cheyenne, hearing his approach, whirled, leapt off the girl as Fargo's blow missed. The man rose, his black eyes grown smaller, and Fargo kept his Colt in its holster. The Cheyenne was alone but shots could bring others. He circled with the Indian as the brave went into a half-crouch, long arms swinging loosely. Out of the corner of his eye he glimpsed Avery scooting backward out of the way, her gray eyes wide.

The Cheyenne feinted, came in with a long, swinging blow, and followed with a lunge, his right arm rocketing forward. Fargo ducked and lifted a long left that caught the Indian's ribs, and he heard the man grunt as he whirled. The Cheyenne came in low again, half-spun, and lashed out with a backhand blow that Fargo just managed to duck. The Indian came around with a long, sideways kick that Fargo managed to take on the side of his thigh; he winced at the force of it. Suddenly, a bone hunting knife appeared in the buck's hand. He must have had it under the back of his loincloth, Fargo cursed silently as he ducked a vicious swipe of the knife, backed, then drew the heavy-barreled Colt. The Cheyenne came in again, ducked low, sprang, and sliced the air with the bone knife again. Fargo pulled his upper body back, feeling the knife graze the front of his shirt. The Cheyenne, off balance at the end of his swiping blow, couldn't recover in time to avoid the barrel of the Colt that smashed against the back of his head.

The Indian stumbled forward as his skull spurted red, and dropped to his knees, managing to half-turn, and Fargo saw him raise the bone knife to throw it. Fargo ducked as the knife flew past him, a wavering throw, and he saw the buck rise and start to lunge at him again. He brought the heavy Colt around in a flat arc and smashed it into the Cheyenne's throat. Fargo felt the impact of throat bones as they broke, splintered, and the Cheyenne made a gargling sound. He was throwing up blood as he fell, quivered, and lay still after one final gargled noise.

Fargo straightened, looked across at Avery Simmons as she watched, her mockingbird-breast gray eyes staring at him. "That makes us even," he growled. He dragged the Cheyenne into the heavy brush behind the shack and returned to see Avery Simmons, who was leading Abel out of the cabin by the hand.

"It's all right now, Abel. It's all over. He's gone," she murmured soothingly as she put the man on the stump, where he sat childlike, head bowed, hands twisted together in his lap. Avery patted his shoulder reassuringly as she met Fargo's eyes.

"You can tell him the real fight hasn't started yet," Fargo rasped.

Her gray eyes narrowed as she retrieved her gun and stuck it into the waistband of her skirt. "You're referring to yesterday, I presume," she said.

"You presume real good," Fargo snapped. "But yesterday's only part of it. I want to know what the hell's going on."

"Daddy insisted I go to town with him yesterday. I couldn't get out of it," the girl said.

"Convenient," Fargo grunted.

"It's true," she insisted. "I did go to the lake as soon as I got free. I saw you and Blythe. You don't waste any time, do you?" He heard the waspishness come into her voice.

"All right, you came to the lake. You wouldn't have come if you didn't figure to talk," he said.

"That was before I realized you and Blythe were so chummy," Avery snapped.

71

"You're real fast at jumping to conclusions," Fargo commented.

The gray eyes darkened in a flare of anger. "My God, I saw you together. You were just dressing and she was still naked as a jaybird. I'm no babe-in-the-woods."

"I don't know what you are, honey," Fargo said.

She put her hands on her hips, and the yellow shirt tightened around full, high breasts and pressed tiny points into view. "Are you really going to stand there and deny what I saw?" she accused.

"Not what you saw, only what you're thinking," he answered calmly. Her eyes stayed, probing, appraising, trying to read behind the chiseled strength of his face. "Who's he?" Fargo asked, nodding toward Abel.

"Someone," Avery returned.

"You're going to come up with better answers than that, Avery, honey," Fargo said tightly.

"Not now. I don't know about you now. I thought you were different than all the others. Now I don't know," she said.

"All what others?" He frowned.

"All the others Blythe Donnen reaches, manipulates, and uses," Avery said darkly. "I have to think about you some more."

"I want to know about you first. What's the disguise and the night-riding mean?" Fargo asked.

"I've my reasons. They don't concern you," she said with sudden loftiness.

"Hell, they don't," Fargo growled. "Are you trying to do something or do you just get your kicks at playing good-deed games?"

"No games, damn you," Avery flung back angrily.

"Then, what?" he pressed.

She flicked a glance at the sun. "I can't talk now. I've got to get back," she said.

"You're not walking away again, honey," Fargo said.

"I'm expected back. I said I was just going for a short ride. I don't want anyone out looking for me. They might spot me coming down from here," she said, and there was real fear in her voice. "Please," she asked. "I'll meet you in the morning. I promise."

"I heard that once before," he said.

"I did come to the lake, damn you," Avery flared instantly. "I was late, but I came."

"So you did," Fargo conceded.

"Where can I find you? I'll come in the morning," she said.

Fargo pursed his lips for a moment. "There are two big cottonwoods that interlock, due east of here," he said.

"I know them," Avery cut in. "I'll be there."

"You better be, or I'm going to bust things wide open when I come for you next," Fargo warned.

She nodded and went to Abel, took him by the elbow, and steered him back to the shack. "I'll be coming soon again, Abel—tomorrow, maybe," she said, and Fargo watched the bald head nod eagerly. "You know what you're to do till I come back," Avery added.

"Think. Try to remember everything," Abel said.

"Very good," Avery answered, and Abel beamed proudly as she led him into the shack. She returned alone in moments and climbed onto the roan.

Fargo swung his horse and rode through the trees after her. They halted when they reached the base of the low hill country, and her gray eyes turned to him, searched his face again, probing. "Thanks for back there, the Cheyenne," she said, unsmiling.

"I owed you," he told her. She accepted the reply and sent the roan on, and he watched her until she went from sight. Avery Simmons was still a mystery package, a lovely creature full of contradictions. But one thing came through: there was no falseness in her. She held back, cloaked herself in silences, but whatever she was up to, she was serious about it. Her dislike of Blythe Donnen was damn plain, too, he smiled. But that could be made of envy or jealousy, Fargo mused, and as Blythe Donnen came into his thoughts, he felt his loins respond at once. He turned the Ovaro north almost automatically as Blythe stayed in his mind.

Maybe she was trying to use him, but that was a game two could play. Meanwhile, she was too much woman not to enjoy. He kept the Ovaro at a steady pace until the ranch came into view, and he spotted Blythe on the brown mare overseeing a calf branding. She spied him approaching, detached herself from the others, and rode to meet him. He saw curiosity in her eyes.

"A surprise visit?" she asked.

"Just to tell you I'll be by for some more convincing tonight," he said.

"Tonight?" She frowned.

"I figured you'd be waiting to try again," Fargo said.

"What if I said I wasn't waiting," she asked.

"I'd say you were lying," he answered as his lake-blue eyes speared her and the tip of his tongue moved across his lips. The surge of smoldering response was quick in her eyes, but her lips tightened.

"Ed and Howard are coming over tonight for a meeting," Blythe Donnen explained.

"Too bad," Fargo muttered. "The way I'm feeling would make last night look like a rehearsal."

"Can you come tomorrow night?" she asked.

He shrugged. "Might not feel the same way then,"

he said. "We'll see." He started to turn the pinto around when her voice called out.

"Wait, I'll give them an excuse, send them home early," she said.

His smile held promise in its slow curl. "I'll see you're not sorry about it," he said, and put the horse into a canter. He rode on, not looking back, and when he was far enough away, he turned the pinto up a small hill and rode back to where the two intertwining cottonwoods rose high over the low hillock. He dismounted under the trees, surveyed the land around him, and tied the Ovaro to a low branch. He walked a dozen or so yards from the two trees to where a thick cluster of snowberry shrubs huddled together. He returned to the Ovaro, took his bedroll, and put it into the thicket of shrubs, lay down on it, and stretched out.

He didn't really mistrust Avery Simmons, but she was still a question mark, and until she became something else, he'd take no chances. He relaxed, dozed off and when he woke, the night was stealing over the hills. He watched the night grow deeper before he finally rose and walked to the trees where the Ovaro waited. He rode from the spot and slowed as he neared the ranch, pulled the Ovaro behind a half-dozen hawthorns as the two riders passed close to him, their voices carrying clearly.

"I'd a lot of things I wanted to go over tonight," he heard Ed Sowerby complain.

"She was tired," Simmons answered.

"I'm tired of you always going along with her. I'm doing things my way," Fargo heard Sowerby reply as his voice faded away. The two riders moved into the night, and Fargo brought the Ovaro from the trees onto the road and cantered to the ranch. The spread was still and dark, only a faint glow of light from the main house. He dismounted, reached the front door as it opened.

Blythe Donnen faced him, naked, her long breasts swaying ever so slightly, the full-thighed legs a few inches apart, the black triangle thrusting forward. Her alabaster skin made her seem almost ghostly in the blackness, and he stepped inside. She pushed the door shut and a lamp turned down low in the corridor cast the only dim light. But he could see her lips open, the tip of her tongue push forward, and he crushed his mouth down over hers, the sight of her instantly inflaming.

He pulled off clothes as he walked beside her to the bedroom, his mouth still on hers, his tongue thrusting deep, circling her own seeking pink organ. He dropped gun belt and trousers in the bedroom as Blythe all but threw herself onto the bed. He followed, came down atop her, and his seeking, pulsating organ found its target immediately as her alabaster thighs fell open for him. He plunged deeply, harshly, and Blythe Donnen's cries filled the room, full-throated cries, each one harsher than the last. Her fingers dug into his back as she pushed against him with his every thrust, and the long breasts fell from one side to the other. He rode hard, felt himself caught up in the vocal ecstasy of her until suddenly her voice became one prolonged sound, and her legs tightened around him. Her climax came with a shriek, her arms pulling his face into her breasts, her legs all but cutting into him, until suddenly she dropped from him, fell back onto the bed, eyes closed, and moaned softly.

"My God, my God," she murmured as he slowly drew from her to lie beside her. He listened to her breathing return to normal, and she moved, came against him, her eyes half-closed as she put her head on his chest. "You've got to stay, Fargo," she whispered. "You've got to stay."

"Convince me some more," he murmured, and she lifted her head, peered at him for a moment.

"Damn you," she murmured, and put her head down again. He guessed not more than three minutes had gone by when he felt her fingers move down his leg, halting, curling around his organ. Blythe Donnen clasped her hand around him, stroked, caressed, and he heard her tiny cries of pleasure as he rose, grew firm, thickened, lengthened under her touch, and suddenly she cried out and her body whirled, came down over his pelvis, and he felt her lips on him, pulling, kissing, drawing in, reveling in the sweet-firm maleness. He heard her murmur between gasps and caresses, and with the same suddenness she flung herself from him onto her back, her hands pulling at his thighs, trying to pull him onto her. "Give it to me, damn you, oh, give it to me," she demanded, and he came over her, plunging hard into her. No subtleties, no sweet savorings of pleasure for Blythe, he had learned. She wanted only the raw, hard crudities of the senses, pleasure at the edge of pain, and again he rode hard with her as her cries seemed to make the walls of the bedroom tremble.

When her final, prolonged shriek signaled the climax for her, he pumped furiously as she grew rigid, and he watched her eyes stare at him as if she disbelieved her own ecstasy. When she finally fell back, fully satisfied, he lay beside her and let silence fill the room. Finally he felt her stir, lift up to rest her breasts on his chest.

"What do I tell the independent's?" he murmured.

Blythe Donnen's head lifted, and the tiny smile that touched her lips was made of triumph. "It seems you've been convinced," she said.

"It seems so," Fargo said carefully. "I just tell them to find their own trail?"

"No, you tell them there's no trail anywhere else," Blythe said. "Tell them to stop poking around looking for what they can't find. Tell them to take what we offer them and be happy."

Fargo kept the smile inside himself. She was completely relaxed, surfeited, off guard, and her quick answer had said more than she realized. Acceptance, that was the important thing to the combine. No one stirring things up—poking around, as she's put it, questioning things as they were. Because finding a new trail might set off finding something more? He turned the question, pushed it into a corner of his mind as he rose and began to pull on clothes. "It's getting late. We don't want your boys to see me leaving at daybreak," he said.

"No, we don't want that. Not yet." Blythe smiled as she stood up, stretched her arms over her head. He amost took off trousers again as the long breasts swayed with sensuous rhythm. He picked up the rest of his clothes as he walked to the front door with her. "When will you tell them?" Blythe asked at the door.

"Soon enough," he said.

"The sooner the better. Don't wait on it," she said, and he smiled at how quickly the tone of authority had returned to her voice.

"I'll be in touch," he said as he left. She closed the door, and he rode quickly from the ranch, heading west, and returned to the two big cottonwoods. He tethered the Ovaro under the trees and strode to his bedroll in the brush, undressed, and lay down. He slept at once, satisfied in more ways than one, and woke when the morning sun flung its hot blanket down. He stayed in the shrubs and pulled only trousers on as the sun blazed with increasing vigor. He felt anger curling inside him as he watched the morning slide almost to a close, and he drew his Colt as she suddenly appeared over the top of the hillock.

He watched her ride under the cottonwoods and slip from the saddle as she peered around the trees. She wore the yellow shirt again, he noted, high breasts tightening the fabric as she moved. "Fargo?" she called, paused beside the Ovaro, glanced around again, and he saw the frown crease her smooth brow. "Fargo?" she called out once more.

He stayed in silence, waited, swept the edge of the hillock with a slow glance. He saw nothing, stood up, the Colt still in his hand.

"Here," he said as he stepped out of the shrubs, and Avery Simmons spun in surprise. But her gray eyes had narrowed as he reached her.

"You're very careful, I see," she remarked.

"That's why I'm still alive," he replied.

Her soft-gray eyes lingered on the muscled beauty of his bare torso before returning to his face. "Do you ever trust anybody?" she asked.

"When they earn it."

"One for you," she said with a wry little smile.

"You're late," he grunted.

"I just managed to get away, and I only came to tell you that something's planned against Ruth Larkin," Avery said.

"What and where?" Fargo questioned.

"I don't know that, but something's planned," she said.

"How do you know?" Fargo questioned.

She hesitated a moment, made a quick face as she answered. "One of our hands. I pay him to tell me things," she said.

"You saying your pa's planned this?" he persisted.

"No. Blythe plans everything," Avery said. "You

can be sure of that. This time they're going after Ruth Larkin. I can't help her, not in broad daylight. I might be recognized."

"This means you've decided to trust me?" Fargo said.

Her eyes flashed. "It means I've no choice," she snapped.

"One for you," he said.

"I guess I'll know if I made a mistake by what you do," Avery said.

"Guess so," Fargo said laconically.

"I'll be back whenever I can get away again," Avery said as she mounted the roan. "It's been hard to get away lately. Daddy's trying to involve me in things around the ranch. I'll wait if you're not here."

"Suit yourself," Fargo said, unwilling to offer her any comfort. "Be ready to do that talking you keep finding ways to avoid," he added. He watched her spin the roan around and ride off at a fast canter, blond hair swinging from side to side. When she was gone, he retrieved the rest of his clothes from the shrubs and left the bedroll there. He dressed and swung onto the Ovaro with a quick glance at the afternoon sky. He set out for Ruth Larkin's modest spread, finally spotted the red cedar out in front, and galloped to a halt in front of the house. A man stepped from the nearby barn, gray-bearded, a battered cap on his head and a sickle in his hand.

"Looking for Ruth Larkin," Fargo said.

"Not here. I'm Jonah. I help out around the place," the man said. "Mighty fine-looking horse you've got there, mister."

"He is that." Fargo nodded. "Where's Ruth?"

"Went to Mountainville with Jess for supplies, like she does every Thursday," the man replied.

"Shit!" Fargo swore as he spun the Ovaro around

and had the horse into a full gallop in seconds. He streaked across low hills and increased speed on the flatlands. Mountainville seemed a terribly faraway place. He had just swung onto the road that led into the north end of town when he saw the buckboard halted in the center of the road. He cursed as he spied the gray dress slumped across the driver's seat, one sack of spilled groceries scattered across the road. He reined the Ovaro to a halt beside the buckboard and swung from the saddle to the wagon, his eyes taking in Ruth Larkin's figure. He saw the red welt at the top of her forehead, but she seemed unharmed otherwise, and he lifted her to a sitting position. She moaned, and he shook her gently as her eyes fluttered open and finally focused on him. She held his gaze for a moment, then pulled her eyes away to glance frantically around her.

"Jess, they took Jess," Ruth Larkin said, and Fargo felt her fingers dig into his arm. "Did you see them?" she asked, turning back to him.

"I didn't see anybody except you," Fargo said. "What happened?"

"They came out from behind those trees over there, all wearing kerchiefs over their faces," the woman said. "Oh, my God, my God. They must've been waiting for us."

"They were," Fargo said. "You go to town to shop every Thursday. How many?"

"I don't know. It all happened so quickly, and they hit me right away. Four, I think ... at least four," Ruth Larkin said. "Why'd they take Jess?"

"To get to you," Fargo said. "They'll be contacting you."

"The bastards, the rotten bastards," Ruth Larkin said, her voice breaking.

Fargo dropped from the buckboard, where the

81

hoofprints led away from the wagon. He studied the marks with his eyes narrowed, reading the tracks as other men read books. Ruth had been right, at least four horses, he guessed, though the hoofprints were bunched together and hard to read.

"Can you drive home alone?" he asked, turning to the woman. "I'm going after them."

He saw the hope explode in her face. "Oh, God, Fargo, you think there's a chance to get Jess?" she asked.

"If there is, I'll bring him back. You get home. We'll talk later," he said, and the woman nodded, casting another quick glance of desperate hope at him as he climbed onto the Ovaro.

"Come back, whatever happens, Fargo," she said.

He waited till she sent the buckboard rolling before turning the Ovaro onto the trail of hoofprints that led north toward the hill country. They'd raced at a full gallop, he saw, and made no effort to hide their tracks. They were figuring that surprise and a fast getaway would be more than enough. Fargo held the Ovaro at a nice, steady, ground-eating pace without pushing the horse, and saw that his quarry had slowed. As they rode up into the hills, they spread out some, and he had a chance to pick up individual horses. Five, he counted as he rode steadily after the tracks. A small and shallow waterway appeared at the bottom of a hill, not big enough to call a river and too big to call a stream. They crossed it, he saw as their prints went into the water, and he followed to the opposite bank, where they made their first attempt at throwing off possible pursuers.

They split up, he saw, three heading north and two going east along the edge of the bank. He leaned out of the saddle as he peered at the two divergent sets of tracks, and his eyes narrowed for a long moment.

When he turned and followed the three horses that had gone north, a grim smile touched his face. Their maneuver would have confused most pursuers. He wasn't one of them. The hoofprints of the two horses that had turned east along the bank were almost identical in depth. If one had been carrying the boy, its prints would have shown the weight of the extra rider.

Fargo spurred the Ovaro uphill after the tracks into terrain that grew thick with trees and brush. But the three riders stayed easy enough to follow as they left a trail of bent branches. He slowed the Ovaro as their tracks suddenly merged into a single file. He proceeded carefully and saw the steep rock formation appear, rise high through the trees. The tracks entered into a narrow defile, wide enough only for a single horse, that appeared in the tall rocks that rose abruptly. Fargo halted and swore silently as he peered at the defile. He didn't like the idea of entering it. It was too easy to be trapped in a defile, and it could end in sudden abruptness that would put him into a hail of gunfire. He scanned the rocks on either side of the narrow defile and saw only unbroken smoothness. He had no damn choice, he swore again, and swung from the saddle, took the Ovaro by the reins, and began to lead the horse into the passage.

He walked slowly, carefully, the Colt in his hand. The defile was already a gray crevice, the late-afternoon sun casting lengthening shadows across the high rock only. He continued to move upward, his gaze fastened on the narrow passage as it led sharply up ahead of him, the rocks steep and smooth on both sides. He had neared the top of the defile, where the sun still touched the rocks when he halted. The shadow reflected against the top edge of the smooth rock, a man's figure perched and waiting at the top of the defile, the silhouette unmistakable. The slender line of a rifle was part of the reflected shadow and Fargo squatted down as he thanked the setting sun's rays, which slanted in a shallow, diagonal angle across the rocks.

His brow creased in thought as he stayed on one knee. They might have gone on ahead and left a third man behind to guard the defile. He rejected the thought as unlikely. They had the boy. They'd stick together. And they weren't really expecting pursuit. His glance traveled up the sides of the defile, but the rocks remained smooth. There was no way to the top except through the narrow pass, and the sentry would spot him the minute he neared the top. He'd have to wait for nightfall, he muttered to himself, and began to back the horse down the defile to the bottom. If they decided to come down, he didn't want to be trapped in the narrow passage. When he reached the entrance to the defile, he moved the Ovaro to one side and settled himself against a birch to wait for darkness.

A twinge of irritation poked at him. The picture was still as distorted, swept with strange undercurrents. Questions were still unanswered and he was still actually uncommitted. Yet here he was in the thick of it. Avery Simmons returned to his thoughts. She held Blythe Donnen responsible for just about everything, her certainty unquestioning. But he had to wonder if she were perhaps very wrong as he thought of Ed Sowerby's remark about doing things his way. Somebody had engineered the taking of Jess Larkin, somebody determined, ruthless, willing to win by any means. He paused in his thoughts. The description partly fit Blythe. Did all of it fit? he wondered. And who else did it fit? he pondered as he thought about Ed Sowerby's crafty eyes.

He put aside further speculation as night finally

came to throw its black blanket across the hills. He rose and began to slowly climb up through the defile again, the Ovaro at his heels. When he had reached the halfway point, he dropped the pinto's reins to the ground, and the horse stood in place as he went on. The soft glow of a small fire drifted into the narrow passage as he neared the top. He dropped to a crouch, crept forward again, and lowered himself onto his stomach as he began to crawl upward. He moved forward with slow, cautious motions, and the form of the sentry at the top of the defile came into sight. Fargo continued to inch his way upward, drawing closer with painful slowness, letting his fingers feel the way. One mistake, one pebble sent clattering down the passage, and he'd be a hopeless target.

When he drew close enough to the top of the defile to see over the edge, he halted, drew in short, silent breaths as he surveyed a small hollow mostly of rock formations that surrounded it with a scattering of heavy scrub brush. A small fire had been set some dozen yards back, the other two men seated before it with the boy between them, his wrists bound. Fargo lay prone, invisible in the blackness, and his eyes swept the scene again. The two men at the fire were half-turned away from him, but he had to take the sentry first, and he speared the man with eyes narrowed almost to slits. The man leaned one shoulder against a tall rock, slouched casually, his back to the defile. He clearly thought he'd hear anyone coming up the passage.

Fargo rose to one knee, then to a crouch. He'd have only one chance. He had to be swift and absolutely silent, no sound to bring the two at the fire up shooting, not a groan, grunt, croak, or thud. He moved forward on steps as silent as a cougar on the prowl, drew his kerchief from his pocket, and held it in his left hand. His right hand took the Colt, turned the butt forward as he came up behind the sentry. He struck with both hands at once, a single, coordinated motion. His left arm circled the man and jammed the kerchief against his mouth as he brought the pistol down hard on the sentry's head. The man started to fall, but Fargo's arm around his neck held him upright until he slowly, silently lowered the unconscious form to the ground.

Fargo looked across at the fire and saw one of the two men turn, peer through the dark toward him.

"Willie'll take over now," the man called, and Fargo saw the second man rise to his feet.

Damn! he breathed silently as the man started toward him. He brought the Colt around. It'd be simple to take the man with one shot, but he held back, finger resting against the trigger. He didn't care for shooting in cold blood, though that had almost cost him his life upon occasion. The circumstances had to be more desperate than these. His Colt stayed aimed at the approaching figure as he raised his voice. "Don't move. Don't do anything stupid," he said evenly.

The man halted, and Fargo heard his gasp of surprise. His glance flicked to the fire where the other man spun around. "Drop your guns, nice and slow," Fargo said, and waited, letting the silence hang in the air. The moment was shattered as the man in front of him went for his gun. Fargo had seen it often enough before, and he was never sure whether it was conceit, fear, or plain stupidity, but the result was usually the same. Fargo's Colt barked and the figure doubled in two as it pitched forward.

Fargo swung the Colt toward the fire, but the other man proved to be smarter. He dived for the boy, rolled, came up with Jess Larkin in his arms. "I'll kill him," the man called as Fargo dropped to one knee, his gun still trained on the man. But the kidnapper had the boy in front of him, and the dim glow of light made an accurate shot impossible. "Drop the gun," the man called out.

"Kill the boy and you're dead," Fargo answered, and moved sideways into the darkest shadows alongside the rocks. "Talk and you can walk," he called.

"Bullshit," the man snarled, and Fargo saw him scoot backward toward where the horses were tied to a clump of brush. "I'm getting out of here and I'm taking the kid. Try to stop me, and he's dead," the man shouted. Fargo edged his way in the black shadows against the rocks, aware that the man couldn't see him. "You hear me, goddammit?" the man shouted.

Fargo remained silent as he moved along the rocks toward the mouth of the defile. The tiny glow of the remaining firelight let him glimpse the man climbing onto one of the horses, yanking the boy up with him. He held Jess against him with one arm as he moved the horse forward and suddenly reined up.

"I know you're out there but you're not goin' to try to sneak a shot at me," the man called.

Fargo continued to stay silent, the mouth of the defile only a few yards away now. But the man took a firmer hold of Jess and stayed in close. "Come out where I can see you," he ordered. "I don't see you, I shoot the kid right now."

Fargo swore inwardly, hesitated, and knew he had no choice. The man fought now with the desperate cleverness of the cornered rat. Fargo took a single step forward, just enough to bring him out of the black shadows where the man could see him. He heard the sound of the horse's hooves as the man spurred the steed on for the mouth of the defile. With his own instinctive alertness, he dropped down and heard the shots explode in the rockbound hollow. Pieces of stone flew into the air as three shots slammed into the rock behind him, and he stayed low as he watched the horse race into the narrow passageway. Not daring to risk a shot, Fargo rose and stretched long legs into a run, racing full speed as he entered the blackness of the defile. He heard the sound of the horse going down the defile ahead of him. It would only be another few moments when the fleeing horseman would find the Ovaro blocking his path, and Fargo continued to race down the steep incline. He heard the sound of the horse skidding to a halt and the man's curse, and kept long legs churning.

The man would have only one choice: dismount, squeeze past the Ovaro, and run on foot. He'd have to leave the boy or slow himself down too much. Fargo came in sight of the big black bulk that was the horses, and kept running. Staying against one wall of the narrow pass, he brushed past the first horse, then the Ovaro, kept going, and heard the man fleeing ahead of him. He was gaining on him, but he slowed, unwilling to catch up in the near-total blackness of the defile. The man was running only a few yards ahead of him now, the sound of his boots clear and close, and Fargo saw the end of the passage just ahead. He drew the Colt as he ran, glimpsed the man as he reached the end of the defile and ran out into the moonlight. Fargo, only seconds behind him, threw himself into a headlong dive at the end of the passage as three shots whistled over his head. He hit the ground, Colt in one outstretched arm, and saw the man where he'd halted, whirled, and fired. Fargo's big Colt answered from where he lay on his stomach, two shots that slammed into their target. The man staggered back once, took another staggered step back, and collapsed as though he were a balloon suddenly deflated.

Fargo pushed himself to his feet, stepped over to the lifeless form, and pushed the man's head into view with the toe of his boot. The man was no one he'd seen, and he turned away and trotted to the defile.

"Jess," he shouted as he started up the passage. "You up there, Jess?"

"Yes," the boy's voice answered, and Fargo trotted upward until he came to the Ovaro. He made out the slender figure moving toward him against one side of the rock wall.

"It's all over," Fargo said. "Take his horse and follow me down." He began to carefully back the Ovaro down the narrow incline until he reached the bottom and the horse had room to turn. He saw Jess Larkin follow him out leading the other horse. "Mount up," he said.

"There are two more horses up there," the boy said.

"They'll pull loose soon enough and make their own way," Fargo said. "Let's move. We've a lot of riding before we get back to your place."

Fargo set an unhurried pace as he traced paths backward under a dim moon. He was grateful for the boy's silence as thoughts tumbled through his head. The three men had been passing faces, maybe hired for the job. Avery had learned about the move against Ruth Larkin. That made it unlikely the distant Señor Arguilla had been behind it. Unlikely, yet not impossible. He could have someone operating close at hand for him. But setting the New Mexico rancher aside for the moment, that left only the good members of the combine. Did they always act together? Fargo wondered. Was Blythe mastermind for everything as Avery Simmons insisted or was she a figurehead for Ed Sowerby's craftiness? Fargo's lips pursed as he thought about Howard Simmons. The man could be hiding ruthlessness behind a mask of blandness. That might explain Avery, Fargo mused. Maybe helping the small ranchers in secret was her way of making up for her father's ruthlessness. It would explain her insistence that Blythe was the guilty one, too.

Fargo toyed with thoughts until he finally set them aside, but not before making one decision. He'd get answers or start to make things happen that'd bring answers. The night had drawn near its end when he reached Ruth Larkin's ranch, a lone light still on in one window of the house beyond the red cedar. He slowed and let Jess race forward, watching as the boy jumped from the horse and ran into the house. Fargo took his time as he dismounted, dropped the Ovaro's reins over the hitching post, and finally walked into the open door. Ruth Larkin was on one knee in front of Jess, holding the boy's hands in hers as he babbled excitedly. "And then he chased the last one down the defile and got him too," Fargo heard Jess recount with wide eyes.

The woman turned as Fargo came into the house, her eyes on the big man that filled the doorway. "You go in, undress, and get some sleep, Jess. God knows you'll need a whole day of it," she told the boy, her eyes still on Fargo. Jess nodded, threw his arms around her again, and hurried from the room. Ruth Larkin stepped to Fargo, her direct brown eyes peering deep into him. "You know I've nothing that can repay you, no words, not anything else, not for what you did," she said.

"Didn't do it to be repaid," he said.

Ruth Larkin's arms lifted, encircled him, and she pressed herself against him. He felt the softness of her deep, full breasts. "I know, and I'll owe you forever," she said. "Maybe some other night you'll come by for the evening."

"You still talking about payment?" Fargo asked not ungently, and she lifted her brown eyes to him.

"No, no paying, just wanting," she said.

"Then maybe I will," he said, then smiled.

"I just thank the good Lord you happened to come by when you did," the woman said.

"It wasn't that way," Fargo said." I just didn't happen by."

A furrow found Ruth Larkin's brow. "What do you mean?" she asked.

"I heard they planned something. I came looking to find you," Fargo said.

The furrow deepened on her brow. "Who told you?"

"You don't know?" Fargo asked sharply as he peered hard at Ruth Larkin. Her frown stayed, and the direct brown eyes stared back at him. She had been through too much these past hours for play-acting, he decided. "I just wondered," he said.

"Who'd be helping us? Why?" Ruth Larkin said, paused, and her frown took on a new dimension. "Is that why you've been thinking we were still holding something back?" she asked.

"Thought about it," he admitted.

Her eyes continued to hold his. "I guess that's understandable," Ruth Larkin said. "Who is it that's been helping us?"

"Can't tell you that—not yet, anyway, not till I know more," Fargo answered.

"But why? I don't understand it," Ruth said.

"That makes two of us," Fargo replied, and turned to leave.

Ruth Larkin's arm went around his waist as she

went to the door with him. "No matter what happens, I'll be owing for always," she said.

"Spend tomorrow with Jess. We'll talk more soon," he said, and walked to his horse. The first streaks of dawn pierced the night sky as he rode from the ranch. There was no one waiting, no roan standing beneath the two trees, and he unsaddled the pinto and felt the tiredness pull at his body. He walked to the shrubs, shed clothes, and lay down on the bedroll and slept instantly as fatigue overtook his body. He turned on his side to ignore the sun when it rose, stayed asleep until he woke rested and refreshed just past mid-morning. He used his canteen to wash, and when he finished dressing, he carried his bedroll back to the Ovaro, which was waiting under the cottonwoods.

He spotted the note then, a square of paper pushed into the pointed end of a low, young branch. He pulled it free, opened it, and read the hastily scrawled handwriting aloud. "I couldn't wait," he read out loud. Three words, he sniffed. No signature, not even an initial. But then it didn't really need that, he conceded. But nothing about returning. She was still avoiding explanations. He crushed the note and tossed it aside. There were other things to get out of the way first, and he saddled the pinto, climbed onto the horse, and rode straight north to where the San Juan Mountains rose up in purple-gray majesty.

6

By midafternoon he was into mountain country, the foothills behind him, and he rode through land heavy with blue spruce and tamarack, longleaf pine and alders, with plenty of hardy mountain brush. Bead-ruby, miners' lettuce, purslane, and peppergrasses formed the main ground cover, none of them worth a damn as food for cattle. He explored, following anything that looked like it might become a usable trail, turned away when it proved unusable, and continued on across the low mountain country. He found only a few moose trails that were good for short distances before they turned off in the wrong direction.

Then he found a wide band of star thistle that a herd could easily trample over, and trailed it to where it ended in a line of rocky plateaus that could be just barely passable. He found narrow trails that meant a herd would have to be stretched out far too long, and passages much too step for a longhorn to climb. When night came, he camped, slept for a short while, and was in the saddle again with the dawn. He came on a few trails that could handle a herd brought through in small numbers, but he'd no way of knowing how far they went without going deeper into the mountains than he planned for the moment. He had set out to explore, survey, make preliminary judgments, not to break trail deep into the mountains. He changed directions and explored other areas of the low range.

But there were more than trails he found. The signs of the Cheyenne were all over, plenty of unshod pony prints, broken Cheyenne arrows, a piece of torn moccasin, the remains of Cheyenne campfires. It was late afternoon when a line of Cheyenne braves appeared on a high ridge and watched him as he rode below until they finally faded silently away into the trees. He was certain there were others who had watched him as he explored. The fact that they were content to let a lone rider move through unbothered was a sign of their strength and confidence. He made camp for one more night and spent the next day riding the lower section of the range, and when the sun began to disappear behind the high peaks, he turned the Ovaro down a narrow path toward the foothills.

He explored a few more trails that appeared as he made his way downward, and he hadn't reached the foothills when night descended. He made camp, enjoyed a good sleep, and continued on down through the lower range when morning came. He cleared the foothills while the sun was still in the morning sky, and rode across the flatland when he saw the rider pulling a yearling along behind him. He recognized Aaron Highbard's narrow frame and steered the Ovaro over to him. The man halted as he rode up and called out a greeting. "Been chasin' this runaway all morning," Aaron said with a nod toward the yearling.

"Get the others together. I'll be at Ruth Larkin's soon after noon," Fargo said. "It's time for hard talk."

"I'll tell them," Aaron said.

Fargo rode on quickly, crossing the gentle low hills

before making his way to the twin cottonwoods. No one was waiting there, but he hadn't really expected there would be. He dismounted, changed his shirt, walked the pinto to a stream, and let the horse drink and cool his ankles. With the sun in the noon sky, he headed for Ruth Larkin's place and saw the small knot of figures outside her house as he rode up.

Ruth Larkin's eyes found him at once, the gratefulness still in them. Armstrong's oxlike figure rested against a seedbed wagon, and the man watched him dismount with truculence in his heavy face.

"I rode the foothills and the low range of the San Juans, the way I said I would," Fargo began as he swept the group with a grim glance. "I don't have anything good to tell you. I don't think you can drive your herds through the mountains. First, the climbing will take too much weight off your steers, especially with no good plains grass for them to feed on along the way. Second, whatever trails I could find will be too hard on cattle and too hard on those trying to keep them together. Third, if the mountains don't do you in, the Cheyenne will. They won't stand still for a herd being driven across their hunting lands."

"You telling us it can't be done, Fargo?" Dennis Toolan asked.

"Can't is a word I don't use much," Fargo answered. "I'm saying I didn't see anything to make me think it can be done." He watched as the others exchanged glances. "Talk it over. You still want to try, I'll take your money and break trail for you. But I'm telling you I don't hold out a hell of a lot of hope."

"You're telling us we have to give in to the combine," Armstrong snapped.

"No, I'm saying maybe there are other ways to find. I can scout the very baseline of the hills. There might be a trail there," Fargo said.

"None that doesn't go onto the combine's land. They saw to that," Armstrong said. "I say I can drive my herd through the mountain country, and I say maybe you didn't look too hard to find us a trail."

Fargo's eyes became blue steel as he fixed an icy stare at Armstrong, and he heard Ruth Larkin's voice cut in.

"You've no cause saying something like that, Armstrong. You're just a bullheaded, sour, suspicous man," the woman said.

"A lucky one, too," Fargo said. "If it weren't for these good folks, I'd push those words back down your throat, Armstrong."

"Don't hide behind these folks," the man said belligerently.

Ruth Larkin stepped forward, her voice rising sharply as she halted in front of Armstrong. "That's enough out of you," she said. "We're all in this together, so you just back off now."

Fargo saw the man's half-sneer as he took a step back. "Maybe some other time, Mister Trailsman," Armstrong said.

"Whenever you want," Fargo answered, and turned his eyes on Ruth Larkin. "Talk it over. I'll come by tomorrow," he said, and Ruth nodded gravely. He rode away as the murmur of voices rose behind him. He turned the horse across the prairie land as the sun edged its way toward the horizon. The thick wheatgrass was made for soft riding, and he finally pulled up onto the distant hillock that let him see the Simmons ranch in fading light. He scanned the spread for a glimpse of blond hair and saw only ranch hands ending the day's chores. Then three figures stepped out of the main house. No blond hair but Blythe Donnen's black tresses contrasted dramatically with her white skin in the dimming light. Ed Sowerby and Simmons walked beside her as they headed toward the horses tethered outside. Fargo watched Ed Sowerby ride off on a gray, Blythe on her dark bay.

The two went their separate ways, Fargo saw with pursed lips as he stayed motionless atop the hillock. There had been a conference, it seemed obvious. A routine meeting or one especially called to talk about the attack that failed? One more unanswered question, he murmured as he moved down from the hillock as night wrapped the ranch in darkness.

He rode back toward the twin cottonwoods as he thought about Blythe Donnen. She'd be wondering about his absence. Angry at it too, for more than one reason. He decided to let her simmer a little longer. He'd other things to settle first. When he reached the cottonwoods, he spread his bedroll and lay down. He stayed awake as long as he could, but fatigue finally closed his eyes. Avery Simmons didn't come, and he wasn't really surprised at that, only angered, and he welcomed the peace of sleep.

When morning came, he retraced steps to Ruth Larkin's place, where Jess was out of the house first to greet him. Ruth followed, her hair hanging loosely, a little curl brushed into it, making her look five years younger. But he kept the smile inside himself. "Take some breakfast with me?" she asked.

"Sounds fine," he agreed, and followed her into the house. She sat him at a bare wood kitchen table loaded with bacon, biscuits, and fresh-brewed coffee. Jess wandered outside, and Ruth Larkin's eyes held on the big man sitting across from her.

"Been thinking about what I said the other night. I keep wondering if it made me seem a loose woman," she murmured.

He reached out and closed his hand over hers on

the table. "No way, Ruth Larkin, not you," he said gently, and saw the quick flood of relief fill her face.

"Good," she said. "Didn't want you thinking that."

He drew his hand back. "You all do your deciding?" he asked.

"More talking than deciding," she answered. "We want to pay you to scout the base of the foothills. We'll decide once and for all when you've done that."

"Fair enough," Fargo said. "Armstrong go along with that?"

"No, but he was outvoted. He left madder'n a wet cat," the woman said.

"Figures." Fargo smiled as he rose to his feet. "Thanks for breakfast. I'll be getting started right away."

"Anytime, Fargo," Ruth Larkin said, putting more than politeness into the words.

"You're looking especially handsome today," he told her, and saw almost a young-girl pride touch her face. She watched him ride away from the doorway, and he waved as he turned the pinto toward the mountain range. He rode directly north until he reached the foothills with the afternoon sun. He had just started to steer the Ovaro along the baseline of the hills when he glimpsed the horse galloping toward him, the sun glinting on the rider's blond hair. He halted and let Avery Simmons catch up to him.

She reined up with a frown of exasperation on her face. "You're a very difficult man to catch up to," she said. "I just happened to catch sight of you when you crossed the last hill."

"You want to leave another note?" Fargo pushed at her coldly.

Her eyes flared instantly. "I couldn't wait that night. I had to leave the note," she said.

"And you couldn't come back the next morning?" Fargo said.

"That's right, I couldn't. It's getting harder and harder to get away," she said.

"Why?"

"Everyone's nervous. Things aren't going smooth. But you know about that," she said.

"You heard, I take it," he said.

"Yes." She nodded. "I'm glad I trusted you that day."

"Compliments?" he queried.

She gave a little half-shrug. She had on a white shirt, a light cotton that rested on tiny little points. "I guess I was wrong about you and Blythe at the lake that morning," she said.

"I told you that," Fargo said blandly.

"I'm sorry. I misjudged you. I owe you an apology," she said.

"You do," he said, and let a note of aggrieved righteousness come into his voice. "Maybe you're wrong about Blythe Donnen too," he suggested.

"No," Avery snapped instantly. "She's behind everything."

"You owe me that explanation you've been avoiding," he said as he slowly rode along the edge of the hills.

"I did come back a few days later. You were gone. I waited as long as I could, but you never showed," she said defensively.

"I'm touched. Talk. Start with Avery Simmons," he said gruffly as he edged the Ovaro past a line of rocks at his right. He swung ahead of Avery's roan as the trail suddenly narrowed for a few yards. He started around a slow curve where it widened again and reined up sharply as he saw the three riders coming around the other end of the curve, one with thick, black hair gleaming in the sun.

"Shit," he hissed, and threw words over his shoulder at Avery. "Stay back," he said.

"What is it?" she asked.

"Company," he said, and snapped a glance at the rocks: two of the closest were tall enough to hide a horse and rider. "Get behind those rocks," he said to the girl. "Quick, dammit." She turned the roan and disappeared into the crevice behind the rocks, and he saw Blythe Donnen suddenly focus on him. He also saw the two riders with her setting claim stakes into the ground at the edge of the foothills. He stayed in place as Blythe sent her horse into a canter toward him. When she reined up beside him, her words echoed the glare she threw at him.

"Where the hell have you been?" she snapped.

"Around," he said mildly. His glance went to the two men that rode up, and he recognized the scar-lipped one and his stringy-haired companion at once.

Blythe dismounted as she barked orders at the two men. "You go on, I'll be along in a minute. Set another stake about twenty-five yards on," she said, and the two men rode on. Fargo swung from the saddle as she returned her attention to him. "Why haven't you come by, dammit?" she hissed, stepping close to him.

"Been away for a few days," he said.

"You tell the others what you decided?" she asked.

"More or less," Fargo said.

Her hand reached up, pressed against his chest, and she shot a quick glance to where the two men were setting down the stake. "Dammit, Fargo, you're habit-forming. I waited every damn night," she said. "I need you again." She drew her hand back. "I can't talk now. You get to my place," she said. "I'll be expecting you." She swung onto her horse and rode quickly to where the two men waited.

Fargo stayed beside the Ovaro until the trio rode from sight. He turned to face Avery Simmons as she strode out from behind the rocks, the roan following, her gray eyes filled with fury.

She swung, a quick, explosive motion, and her hand just grazed his face as he pulled back. "Bastard," she hissed. "Lying bastard. I was right all along."

"No, you weren't," he said calmly.

"You've been sleeping with her. You lied to me," Avery shouted. "I asked you, and you lied about it."

"You asked about that morning at the lake," Fargo said. "I told you the truth about that."

"What about the nights she mentioned?" Avery threw back.

"You didn't ask about them," he returned mildly.

"A half-truth's the same as a lie," she said. "Damn you, I was just beginning to trust you."

"Just hold your damn tongue, honey," Fargo flared. "You're a hell of a one to talk about half-truths. You've been living a half-truth, playing night rider, hiding a dopey old man in a shack. What the hell are you all about?"

"You want to know what I'm all about?" Avery echoed as she swung onto her horse. "I'll tell you, but not here. Your girlfriend might come back." She sent the roan into a gallop, and Fargo climbed onto the Ovaro and chased after her. He made no effort to catch her as he rode a few yards back. She headed into the low hills, and when he entered the thick, lush terrain, he knew where she was headed. He rode into the little hollow with the shack in it a few moments after she reached it. He was dismounting as she strode into the shack. He heard her talking to Abel inside the shack and settled himself on a log until she came out alone, her gray eyes instantly finding anger as she saw him.

"I'm waiting," he said.

She walked to the log, drew a deep breath, and sat down beside him. There was still anger in the quick glance she threw at him, but there was something else, a sudden flood of weariness. "I thought maybe you'd make the difference," she said. "Now I don't know anymore."

"What difference?" Fargo asked.

"The difference between having a chance to win and not having one," Avery said, anger returning to her voice. She turned, her gray eyes studying him with a deep furrow in her brow. "How could you?" she asked. "How could you sleep with her, a woman without any principles?"

"We haven't gotten to principles yet. We're still on pussy," he answered.

"You're impossible," Avery Simmons snapped. "You enjoy being crude."

"Sometimes truth is crude. You're poking and prying. You just want sugarcoated answers, honey," Fargo said. "Why are you helping the small ranchers against your father?"

"My father's a man who's been hypnotized, trapped, and used," Avery said.

"By Blythe Donnen," Fargo supplied.

"Yes," Avery almost shouted. "You're a perfect example. She has my father thinking she's being pure as the driven snow waiting for him, and she's busy giving out with you and God knows who else. But it's more than that. She's got him doing things he'd never do on his own, agreeing to things he'd never agree to if he wasn't spellbound, bewitched."

"Maybe you'd just like to think it's because of that," Fargo slid at her.

She halted, blinked, took in his words. "No," she answered after a moment. "I know my father. He wouldn't be trying to do in the small ranchers. He never did before, not until Blythe got her hooks into him."

"What about Ed Sowerby? He bewitched too?"

"He's just a little weasel who's convinced Blythe can bring it off, and he wants to be on the winning side," Avery said.

Fargo turned her words about her father in his mind. He'd seen men bewitched by women before, captured body and soul, turned into putty. Simmons could well be one of them. "What about this New Mexico rancher, Arguilla?" Fargo asked. "According to Blythe, he's the one had me set up in Ten Rocks."

"Is that what she told you?" Avery frowned, and a wry smile touched her lips. "Arguilla's a tired, old man who wouldn't hurt a fly. He doesn't even care about outside cattle coming in. He has his own markets."

Fargo probed at her with his eyes. She'd thrown most everything out with no careful choosing of words. But he wanted another answer. "You've been trying to help the small ranchers. You care about their problems?" he questioned.

"Frankly, no," Avery said. "I don't really give a damn about the small ranchers. I'm helping them because I want Blythe Donnen stopped. If she fails, she'll clear out, and my pa will see her for what she is."

Fargo nodded at her honest words, no attempt to paint a false picture about herself. She had the kind of self-honesty that was hard to come by. "You have anything but words about all the things you say about Blythe? Any proof of anything?" he asked.

"I've been trying to get proof," Avery said. "Something's wrong about all that she's doing, about the whole scheme she has my pa caught up into. Only I can't put my finger on it. She's so damned clever."

"Is that where Abel comes in?" Fargo asked, and Avery nodded.

"Abel knew something. He was going to pull the plug on it. He was on his way someplace to do it when they stopped him and killed him. Or they thought they did. I got there just after they left him for dead. I saw he was still alive, though they'd shot him in the head, and I took him to the cabin," Avery said. "I nursed him every day for weeks. The bullet had passed clean through his head, and he finally came around."

"Only he's half a vegetable," Fargo said.

"The bullet must've hit something that contols the memory part of the brain. But he's been making slow progress. Every week he seems to remember a little more. God, I keep working with him, trying to bring him back. Maybe it's a waste of time. Maybe there's too much damage," Avery said as she pushed herself to her feet and paced back and forth.

"Or maybe it'll take too long before he can really put it all together," Fargo said.

She nodded gravely, her lips growing tight. "Yes, I've thought of that. But I have to keep trying."

"How'd you come to be there just after he was shot?" Fargo asked.

"Abel and I used to talk. He knew I was concerned. He told me he knew some things, but he wouldn't tell me any more. He said that I'd be safer not knowing but that he'd handle it," she said.

"So nobody knows you have him stashed away up here," Fargo said.

"Nobody, except you now," she said.

"If they find out, they'll finish the job, and maybe you too," Fargo said. "If what you say about Blythe

Donnen is right, you've been playing a damn dangerous game."

"It is right. You keep on saying if," Avery flared at him. "She'd kill you as quickly as she screwed you. Is that plain enough?"

"That's plain enough." Fargo half-smiled. "But why do you keep sounding more jealous than concerned?"

He saw the question take her aback, almost as though she'd been struck a physical blow. Her gray eyes clouded as she stared at him. "Maybe I am jealous," she said slowly. "I'm jealous of the way she looks, of her cleverness, her confidence in herself, of the way she can wrap people around her little finger, especially men."

Fargo smiled thoughtfully, her answer more of the same inner honesty she had shown before. "Jealousy never gets you anyplace," he said.

"Nothing else does," Avery snapped angrily. "I'm still not really sure about you, even though you did help Ruth Larkin."

"And I'm not sure about everything you've said. You've a lot of words and accusations about Blythe," Fargo returned. "I want something more than words."

"I don't have proof. I don't need it," Avery threw back.

"I do, and maybe I can get enough to answer some things," Fargo said.

"How?" she asked.

"My own ways," he said, and she frowned at him, deciding she'd get no further answer. "You've no idea what Abel had locked up inside him or where he was going that day they hit him?" Fargo questioned.

"No," Avery said, and her shrug was one of helplessness.

"Who'd he work for, your pa, Sowerby, or Blythe?" Fargo asked.

"None of them. He worked for Thomas Boyard," Avery said.

"Boyard?" Fargo frowned and pulled the name from his mind. "I met him at your pa's affair, chief clerk of the land survey office, right?"

"Right," Avery said, nodding.

Fargo's lips pursed as a flood of unformed thoughts exploded inside him. "You ever see claim deeds to all the land the combine owns?" he asked.

"Yes, Daddy has a copy of every claim deed. So do the others," Avery answered. "That shoots down that thought. I had the same one when Abel was attacked."

"Maybe, and maybe not," Fargo muttered as he frowned into space.

"I told you, I saw them. They were shown to all the small ranchers too. They exist," Avery said unhappily.

"Abel worked for Boyard in the land survey office. There has to be some connection," Fargo said.

"I don't know what it could be," Avery said.

"I'll work on it," Fargo said as he glanced up at the sky, which had begun to gray. "Shouldn't you be getting back? It's a fair ride from here, and you want to be careful you're not seen."

"I can't go back tonight. I said I was staying with Judy Conners over in Greenvale for the night. If I go back now, there'll be questions, and I'm not up to questions tonight. I'll sit here till morning," Avery said.

"You share the cabin with Abel?"

"No, I stay outside. I tried that once when I was working hard with him. He did nothing but stare at me all night, just stare and stare. I couldn't stand it. I slept out here," she said.

"Maybe I'll come back later. Might think of some

more questions for you," Fargo said as he walked to the Ovaro.

"Where are you going now?" Avery frowned.

"Pay a visit to Blythe. I told you I want proof," he said. "I'm going to get it."

"By sleeping with her again?" Avery shot back. "That's a new approach, I must say. Questions between quivers? Is that how you're going to get your proof?"

"You're sounding jealous again, honey," Fargo observed.

"Go to hell," she flung back as he climbed onto the Ovaro and rode away.

He'd learned from their first meeting that she had a tart tongue. It was more so when fed by anger, hurt, and he still wagered, some jealousy that was purely female. But he found himself admiring her as he rode through the night. Not nearly so sure of herself as she let on, she was nonetheless willing to fight single-handedly for her own convictions, stick her neck out, become a night rider, take all the risks of being caught. She had to believe she was right to do it, he reflected. But her belief wasn't enough for him. He had to have proof, something more than inner convictions that could be misdirected.

When he finally reached Blythe's ranch, he rode to the house through silent darkness, only the distant bellow of a steer breaking the stillness. He dismounted, rapped softly on the door, and waited. She took a few minutes to answer, and when she opened the door, she held a silk gown around herself. He saw her eyes instantly take on irritation along with welcome.

"Come in," Blythe Donnen said. "You're late."

"Can't stay," Fargo said, and saw the irritation deepen in her eyes at once. "Just came by to tell you something. The small ranchers have called in a hired gun. His name's Conway."

Blythe frowned at once. "Now, why would they do that?" she questioned.

"Guess they figure on fighting back," Fargo said casually. "I just thought you'd like to know."

"Well, of course, I always like to know something like that," Blythe said. "You know anything else about him?"

"Only that he's due to be at the hotel in Mountainville tomorrow night," Fargo said. "I overheard that much."

Blythe nodded and opened the door wider. "Why can't you stay?" she asked.

"They owe me some traveling money. I'm to pick it up tonight," he said.

Her hand reached out to curl around his arm. "You won't be needing their traveling money. You'll make plenty more with me. Come in," she said.

He shook his head. "They agreed to traveling money. I'll hold them to it. Matter of principle," he said, stubbornness in his voice.

She let a moment pass. "All right, I guess I understand," she said, and her voice grew authoritative at once. "But don't disappear for days again. I don't like it."

"I won't," he said as he backed from the doorway and swung onto the pinto. He heard her close the door quickly as he rode away. He had put out the cheese. Now he had only to wait and see. If she bit at it, he'd have his proof. If she didn't, then maybe Avery was all wrong about the woman. Blythe's reactions to the information he'd dropped in her lap had told him nothing. He had to wonder whether that meant innocence or cleverness. He spurred the horse into a trot and pushed away further speculation. He'd have that much answered soon enough.

He rode under a half-moon as he moved up into the low hills, and he felt the night turning cool on a gusty wind. When he reached the thick, lush trees, he threaded his way carefully, watching for places he'd marked in his mind, and finally rode into the small hollow where the shack sat at one edge, its sagging roof outlined in the pale light. The moon also outlined the figure sitting against a tree trunk, arms folded around herself. He saw a shiver course through her as he dismounted.

"Why don't you get into your bedroll instead of sitting there getting cold?" He frowned.

"Didn't bring one," she answered, and he stared at her. "I said I was staying with Judy. Why would I take along a bedroll?"

"All right," he said. "But you'll get yourself pneumonia sitting out here. It's turning right chilly tonight. Get in the shack, at least."

"No, I tried that again. I just can't stand his staring at me," she said. "I'll be all right out here."

"Hell you will," he said, turned to the Ovaro, and pulled his own bedroll free. He tossed it down in front of Avery. "Use this. Get inside before you turn blue," he ordered.

Her gray eyes held on him gravely. "Where are you going to sleep?" she asked.

"Same place," he said.

"Oh, no, no. Then I'm certainly not using that bedroll," she said.

"You'd rather get yourself sick," Fargo commented.

"Yes, anytime, rather than sleep next to someone who's just been sleeping with Blythe Donnen," Avery flared. "Did you get your proof?" she added with waspishness.

"Not yet," Fargo said calmly.

"All fun and no answers? What a shame," she slid at him, each word wrapped in sarcasm.

"If you say so," Fargo remarked.

"You're being tricky again," Avery accused.

"You're asking and answering all by yourself," Fargo said.

"You didn't sleep with her tonight?" Avery snapped. "That's a direct question."

"No. That's a direct answer, not that it's any of your damn business," Fargo barked.

Her eyes held him, peered hard, and in them he saw the desire to believe him. He saw something more too—pain, uncertainty, and a kind of lostness—and he felt suddenly sorry for her.

"That's the truth," he told her, and took the hardness from his voice. He reached arms up and began to pull off clothes. "Now, I'm chilly and tired, and I'm going to get myself a nice, warm sleep. You can be as stiff-backed and stupid as you like, honey," he said. He stripped down to the bottoms of his underwear, and her eyes stayed on him, took in the muscled beauty of his body as he slid into the bedroll.

She stayed standing above him, the edge of a pout on her lips. A sharp gust of wind sent a shiver through her, and she took a step toward the bedroll. "You promise not to try anything?" she asked.

"You promise not to touch me, and I won't touch you," Fargo said blandly.

"Very funny." She sniffed. "Move over."

He slid himself to one side of the bedroll as she started to sink to her knees and climb under the top cover. "You going to sleep in your blouse and skirt?" he asked.

"Of course," she said almost indignantly.

"How are you going to explain why your clothes are

so wrinkled from spending the night at your friend's house?" he mentioned, and saw her stop, frown, her lips tighten.

"Dammit," she muttered.

"Be kind of hard to explain that," Fargo commented.

"Yes," she said, and her hand went to the buttons of her blouse. "You just going to lie there and stare?"

"I said I wouldn't touch. I didn't say I wouldn't look," he answered.

"Damn you," Avery snapped, swung herself into the bedroll, and turned her back to him as she maneuvered to pull off the blouse and the skirt. She had to sit up to fold them neatly on the ground beside the bedroll, and he glimpsed the side of one lovely full breast and a nice broad back before she settled in and pulled the cover over her. He lay back and listened to her turn restlessly.

"Never get any sleep that way," he murmured.

"I'm not exactly used to doing this," Avery said.

"Maybe it's time you got used to it," Fargo said.

"Oh, sure. I'm supposed to get used to sleeping near naked in a bedroll with someone I don't know if I can really trust or not," she returned.

"Adds extra spice, I'd say," Fargo remarked. "Settle down and tell me about Avery Simmons."

"There's not much to tell," she said.

"Avery's a boy's name, isn't it?" he asked.

"Usually. My father wanted a boy, had the name all picked out. When I came along, I got it anyway," she said. "Mother died about ten years ago, and I've been running the house ever since."

"You think it's your job to save Daddy from other women?" Fargo prodded.

"No, and that's a rotten thing to say," Avery flared instantly. "It's not other women. It's Blythe Donnen."

"Simmer down," he soothed. "I believe you." She made a small sound of acceptance. "You know, honey, you could lose while you win," he said gently.

"Meaning what?"

"Daddy might not be overjoyed at your ripping his love into pieces. You don't just turn off being bewitched," Fargo said.

"I've thought of that. I have to take that chance," she said.

"There's more," Fargo told her. "What if your pa's into this a lot deeper than you think? It could turn real nasty, and Blythe won't be the only one hurt."

She was silent for a long moment. "It won't turn out that way. I just know it," she answered finally, and he let her hang on to that hope. Hell, he'd nothing better to give her. He wasn't even convinced she was right about Blythe.

"Get some sleep," he said gruffly, and heard her turn on her side.

"Good night," she said softly.

He lay on his back, but stayed awake, reminding himself that he'd promised not to touch. He told himself not to make promises like that again as he turned on his side and closed his eyes.

7

Fargo slept heavily, using sleep as a refuge to shut out thoughts of Avery's young, curvacious body only six inches away from him. It was nearing dawn when the sound of scurrying feet near the bedroll woke him and he saw a pair of martens hurrying by. They disappeared into the brush. Awake now, he felt the softness against him, turned his head to see Avery hard asleep, but she had slid against him. Her round, soft little rump was warm through the thin fabric of the bloomers where it rested against his leg. She slept half on her stomach, knees partially drawn up and one arm flung out where it rested against his shoulder, the position little-girl-like. He smiled and returned to sleep until the morning sun woke him. He stayed unmoving and let her wake, felt her pull away instantly, and heard the sharp intake of her breath. He felt her peer at him to see if he knew she'd been lying against him, and he continued to feign sleep. Satisfied that he hadn't, he heard her rise, slip out of the bedroll, and move away.

He opened his eyes and caught a glimpse of her bloomer-covered round rear disappearing into the trees, and he stretched and sat up. He emerged from the bedroll slowly, scanned the hollow, and saw nothing to give him alarm. He was still in his underwear bottoms when she returned, the blouse and skirt on but her face still glistening with droplets of water. "I expected you'd have some clothes on by now," she said reprovingly, though he saw her eyes stayed on his muscled body.

"You expected wrong, honey," he said.

"There's a stream just beyond the shack," Avery said as she fished a hairbrush from her saddlebag.

He rose, took a towel and trousers with him as he walked away and felt her eyes stay on him. He found the stream, washed in the cold, refreshing water as he scanned the hillsides out of habit. Only a red-winged blackbird broke the stillness, and when he finished washing, he dried himself and pulled on trousers and gun belt. When he returned to the hollow, Abel was outside of the shack, munching on biscuits as Avery sat beside him. Her eyes lifted as Fargo approached, and he saw the discouragement in the gray depths.

"He's not responding at all today," Avery said. "He's not remembering the things he did last time." She rose and paced back and forth, her arms folded across the full, high breasts. "Times like this I think maybe it's all been a waste. I wonder if he'll ever remember anything more than he has," she said.

"Maybe it's time to stop with Abel and start with where he worked," Fargo said.

"The land survey office?" Avery frowned.

"I still say there's some connection," Fargo said.

"I told you I've seen the claim deeds," Avery said. "So have others."

"I'd like to see them for myself," Fargo said.

She frowned into space for a moment. "Maybe I can sneak you into the house at night, after everyone's asleep," she said. "Daddy keeps them in the study desk."

"I don't want to see those. I want to see the ones in the land survey office. I'm going to get in there and have a look at them," Fargo told her.

"I can help. I'll go with you," Avery said.

"I work better alone," he said.

"I worked for Tom Boyard for two summers when I was younger. I know the office. I know what he keeps where," Avery said. "When do we do it?"

He considered her words. Time would be important, he realized. Having someone who knew the inside of the office would help. "I don't know yet. Keep in contact, and I'll tell you," Fargo said.

"All right," Avery agreed. "It's time I started for home." She walked to where Abel sat amid the crumbs of his biscuits, and gently pulled the man to his feet, walked back to the shack with him as she guided his steps. "You try to remember more, Abel," Fargo heard her say as she took the man inside the shack. "I'll be back tomorrow. Meanwhile, you keep trying, you hear, Abel?"

Fargo waited until she came from the shack and hurried to the roan, her face set tightly. Her eyes met his as she climbed onto the horse.

"Thanks for the use of the bedroll," she said.

"I enjoyed it." Fargo smiled. "Especially that nice, round, warm little rear that slept against me." He almost laughed as her cheeks grew beet-red and she whirled the roan around and raced away, blond hair flying. She vanished into the trees, and Fargo lowered himself against a birch, plans already forming in his mind. When he'd finished, he rose and went to the door of the shack.

Abel sat in a straight-backed chair, oblivious to the figure in the doorway, a vacant half-smile on his face.

Fargo backed from the doorway, shook his head grimly as he saddled the Ovaro. He had little confidence Abel would tell Avery anything more than he had, which was almost nothing. When the Ovaro was saddled, Fargo rode out of the hollow, through the lush hillsides, and when he reached the flatland, he turned the horse toward Mountainville. He rode slowly through town to the hotel, turned down a side street, and left the Ovaro at the rear of the hotel.

He walked back to the front door and stepped into a small lobby, where an elderly, stooped man greeted him from behind the front desk. "Name's Conway. I want a room on the ground floor with a window," Fargo said.

"Got one left," the man said, and Fargo tossed him a silver half-dollar as he scribbled the name "Conway" in the register. He took the key the clerk handed him, went down the main-floor hallway, found the room, and closed the door behind him. He swept the room with a slow eye that missed nothing. The window looked out onto a side street with a corner of Main Street barely visible. A single bed rested against the wall across from the window, and a tall closet took up part of the opposite wall. He opened the closet, stepped inside it, and let the door hang open. It allowed him a clear view of most of the room, the window the only thing out of his line of vision. Stepping out of the closet, he closed the door and checked the window. There was no hatch, he noted with satisfaction.

When he left the room, he hurried past the elderly desk clerk, went down the side street to the rear of the hotel, and swung onto the Ovaro. He stayed out of town and cut directly across from the hotel, over a field of tall sedges until he went into tree cover. He rode on a half-mile farther and halted where a nest of gray birch formed a ragged arch. He slid to the ground, sat down against one of the birches, and relaxed, dozing some in the little glen, as he listened to the sounds of cowbirds and tanagers.

He rose as the light began to dim, and scouted through the woods until he found a piece of birch log about five feet in length, almost two feet in diameter, and knobby at one end. He lifted it onto the saddle as night fell, and held it in front of him as he rode slowly back toward Mountainville. He halted where the trees did, tethered the Ovaro out of sight, and carried the log on his shoulder as he walked to the rear of the hotel, made his way along the narrow side street to the window of the room he'd rented.

He opened the window, slid the log inside, and followed it into the room. He closed the window behind him at once. The room was dark and he let his eyes grow accustomed to the almost-pitch-blackness. A dim glow of moonlight filtered its way in through the window, and he carried the log to the bed, pulled the covers back, and laid the knobby end near the pillow. He fluffed the bedcovers up around the log and stepped back, surveyed his work. In the darkness of the room, the bed seemed to have someone asleep in it. It was one of the oldest tricks, he realized, but it continued to work at the right time and the right place, and he was confident this was one of those instances. He backed from the bed, satisfied with his deception, and opened the closet, and stepped inside. Leaving the door open, he lowered himself to the floor in the total blackness inside the closet. It would be a long wait, he was certain. Anyone who came would wait for the night to grow long, and Fargo sat back against the closet wall, let his body relax as he pulled calm patience around himself as if it were a cloak. He had long ago learned what most men never learn but what every wild creature knows instinctively: waiting is but another part of action.

The street sounds that drifted into the room through the window—the creak of wagons, the tattoo of hooves, and the dim voices of men—began to grow still finally as the night lengthened. Fargo continued to relax inside the closet when suddenly he sat up, every muscle tensed instantly. The sound had come from the window, a tiny scraping noise as the window was slowly lifted and rubbed against its dry wood frame. The sound stopped, then came again. Whoever it was used caution, lifting the window only inches at a time, until Fargo heard the sound of legs being pulled across the windowsill.

He remained motionless, hardly breathing, as the figure came into sight, a dark shape crossing the room to the door. The man opened the door slowly, just enough to let two more figures slip into the room. Fargo slid the big Colt from its holster, his lips tight. It had gone just as he expected it would so far. They had asked for Conway's room at the desk clerk, and two had gone to wait at the door while the third made his way to the window. As he watched, the three men took up positions a few feet apart, faced the bed, completely unaware of his presence in the blackness of the closet. At a hand signal, they pulled six-guns and poured a torrent of bullets into the shape on the bed. The bedcovers fluttered and jounced as the slugs tore through them, and ending together, the three figures stopped shooting and stepped to the bed. One yanked the covers back and Fargo heard his curse of surprise.

"Drop your guns," Fargo said quietly. "Don't be stupid." The last piece of advice fell on deaf ears as the trio whirled, brought their guns up to fire. The figure at the very left got off two wild shots. The other two never fired as Fargo's Colt barked and both figures fell, one to the floor facedown, the other half across the bed. His hand clutched the bedcovers and pulled them down with him as he slid to the floor. The third man tried to race for the door.

"Hold it right there," Fargo shouted. The man ignored the command, reached for the doorknob. His hand was around the knob when Fargo fired two shots. They slammed into the man, flung him against the door. He slid slowly downward to the floor, his one hand still curled around the doorknob.

Fargo stepped from the closet, walked to the two figures beside the bed, and realized he had mixed feelings as he stared down at them. Using the toe of his boot, he turned the nearest one on his back and saw a trickle of red running from the man's mouth. It ran down the left side of his face and left the scarred lip clearly visible.

"Shit," Fargo murmured softly, pushed the other figure on its side. The man's hat fell off, and long, stringy hair tumbled across his face. Fargo turned away, his mouth a tight line. He'd seen enough. He stepped to the windowsill, lifted himself over it, and dropped to the ground outside. The desk clerk would have run for the sheriff at the furious hail of shots, and Fargo loped down the side street and across the sedges until he reached the Ovaro in the trees. He swung onto the horse and rode through the trees, a bitter taste in his mouth.

He had set the trap, put out the bait, and Blythe had taken it, sending her two gunhands and one more to do her bidding. He had one answer now. Blythe Donnen was much more than an ambitious, determined woman. It was plain that she'd engineered the setup to kill him back at Ten Rocks. All the other attacks that had taken place too. She planned killings as other woman planned parties. She was ruthless, amoral, a beautiful serpent. And wonderful in bed. He thought of her wild cries in the night. It was the one time and place she was not in control of herself, and his lips formed a harsh smile as his thoughts raced. He'd a few things to tell Blythe Donnen. What better place, what better time, and what better way than in bed.

He sent the pinto into a trot as dawn touched the sky. He finally halted under the twin cottonwoods, and after unsaddling the pinto, he took his bedroll into the brush and slept quickly into mid-morning. He rose, dressed slowly, and foraged some until he found a stand of sweet pears. He stayed the day near the cottonwoods and used the time to plan ahead. After Blythe, the land survey office was next, with or without Avery's help. When the afternoon deepened, he rose and rode to Ruth Larkin's place. She hurried from the house to greet him.

"Where's Jess?" he asked.

"Out riding the fields. I don't want to keep him so close to home he becomes fearful of going out on his own," she said, and smoothed a straying lock of hair back with one hand. "I thought you might have come by one of these evenings," she said with just the faintest hint of disappointment in her voice.

"Things got in the way," he said. "But I thought about it," he added, and caught the tiny glint of satisfaction in her eyes.

"You come with answers?" she asked.

"No, but soon," he said. "Maybe different than the kind you're expecting."

"The others are getting very restless. We ought to be starting to drive cattle now," Ruth Larkin said.

"Tell them to be patient a little longer," Fargo told her.

"How much longer?" she asked.

"Another few days," Fargo said.

"I'll try, but you've got to tell us yes or no by then. You taking us through or not," she said with finality.

"I'll take you through, one way or the other. You can tell them that," he said.

"Meaning what exactly?" she pressed.

"If there's no way through the high mountains and none around the baseline, I'll figure out something else," he said.

She nodded thoughtfully. "That'll help hold them a little longer," she said.

He nodded, turned the horse, and left as dusk spread itself across the land. He rode slowly, let the half-moon rise high before he made his way to Blythe Donnen's ranch. He dismounted outside the darkened house and rapped softly on the door. She answered after a moment, stared at him with a frown. She wore a deep-red silk dressing gown, floor-length, that clung to her figure. The deep, alabaster-white breasts rose upward invitingly. She was a striking creature, he admitted inwardly, jet hair and jet eyebrows against the white skin. But the coral snake was beautiful too. So was the pitcher plant.

"Come in," she said almost crossly. "I never know whether to expect you these days."

"Not much welcome in that, honey," Fargo commented.

"It's been a bad day. Nothing seems to go right lately," she muttered darkly.

"Such as?" he asked with casual innocence.

"Different things," she said, dismissing the question. "But I'm smelling a rat someplace."

"What kind of rat?" he tried.

"I'm not sure. Could be a female rat," Blythe said. "But that's none of your concern."

"I know what you need," Fargo said, and stepped

closer to her. "Some late-night delight. Best thing for forgetting your troubles."

"I don't know. I'm not in the mood," she said.

"I am," Fargo said, reached out, his hands sliding inside the deep-red silk material to cup both full breasts, his thumbs pressed into the pink-brown tips.

"Oh, God," Blythe Donnen gasped, and Fargo pressed upward with both hands, pushed the deep breasts together. Blythe gasped again, and he felt her body quiver. "Oh, what the hell," she murmured as she turned and walked to the bedroom, his hands still cupped around her breasts. She lifted her shoulders and arms, and he took his hands away as she slipped the dressing gown off. Fargo stepped back and shed clothes. She threw herself onto the bed, spun onto her back, all thirsting hunger, the curly triangle thrust upward, so very black against the white of her slightly rounded belly and full thighs. He lay half over her, his mouth finding one breast, and she gave a short cry at once. He let his hand slide down through the dense, curly triangle, cup against the warm portal. She was already moist, warm wetness flowing in the eternal welcome. He let his hand press deeper, move over the serous lips, and she let out a little scream. He turned atop her, pressed the tip of his pulsating, seeking organ against the warm wetness, and her cries began, one atop the other as he moved inside her with harsh, driving thrusts.

"Oh, oh, yes, yes," she managed between her wild cries, and as he drove harder and faster, her cries became piercing and her full-fleshed body throbbed and heaved. Suddenly, as her cries filled the room, he felt her thrusting, heaving body begin to quiver. "Yes, yes, now, now, more," Blythe Donnen screamed as the genesis of ecstasy began to take hold.

Fargo, the effort wrenching, lifted and pulled himself from her. "Can't," he murmured as her hands clutched at his shoulders.

"No, God, no. What are you doing?" she screamed in angry protest. "Goddamn, come back!"

"No, can't," he repeated as she flung herself at him, trying to wrap her legs behind his back and pull him forward.

But he half-twisted, and her legs slipped down. He saw her staring at him, a mixture of fury, helpless frustration, and strange disbelief in her eyes.

"Come back, goddamn you. Why are you stopping?" she hissed.

"Have to." He shrugged.

"You can't, goddammit, you can't," Blythe cried out as she tried again to wrap legs and arms around him. Once again he twisted away, swung from the bed, and started to pull on trousers. Blythe sat up, aghast. "What are you doing, goddammit? What the hell's wrong with you?" she demanded. "You can't leave me like this."

"It wouldn't be right to stay," he said apologetically. "It's a matter of principle."

Blythe Donnen continued to stare at him, but he saw rage pushing everything else out of her eyes now. "What the hell are you talking about?" She frowned.

"Keeping my word," he said with a half-smile he laced with ruefulness. "The small ranchers. Guess it's been a habit for too long."

"You bastard," Blythe screamed as she swung alabaster white legs over the edge of the bed. "You stinking bastard."

He let himself look hurt. "I didn't think you'd want to get screwed both ways," he said mildly.

"Bastard," she screamed, standing to face him, her face growing red with rage.

"That hired man I told you about?" Fargo said. "I

123

took his place last night. Turned out to be sort of like a turkey shoot."

Blythe's hand swung out, fingernails outstretched to rake across his face, and he just managed to pull back in time. "I'll kill you," she screamed in utter fury.

"You tried that, honey," Fargo said as he caught her wrist, twisted, and flung her facedown onto the bed. He brought his open palm down with all his strength on her rear and saw the alabaster skin turn instant red as she screamed.

He stalked across the room, yanked the door open, and a quick glance back showed her beautiful, naked form turning, taking hold of a small vase on a nearby end table. He heard it crash into bits against the door as he pulled it closed and trotted from the house, her muffled shouts following. He rode from the ranch at a fast canter and slowed only when he reached the prairie land, his lips a thin, hard line.

He'd flung the gauntlet down and she'd waste no time reacting, he was certain. But that didn't bother him. It was her remark about a female rat that bothered him. She had plainly been brooding about too many plans going awry and had begun to put two and two together. Too smart not to be aware of Avery's dislike, she'd started wondering about Avery's role, and that meant the girl could be in real danger. But there was a little time yet, he realized, enough to warn Avery, he hoped. Blythe wouldn't move openly or hastily against Howard Simmons' daughter. She couldn't afford that yet. But if Avery didn't show in the next few days, he'd go seek her out, he knew.

He reached the cottonwoods, unsaddled the Ovaro, and slept fitfully in the nearby brush until he decided to get up with the morning sun. He'd finished dressing, saddled the Ovaro, when he saw the distant horsemen riding hard across the flatland. They stayed apart and rode in a long circle they made in opposite directions. He mounted the Ovaro and rode out from beneath the cottonwoods, concentrated on the nearest rider, and strained his eyes until he recognized Ritchie Thornton. The youth saw him at almost the same instant and turned his horse to gallop toward him. Fargo waited, letting the youth come up, and saw that the other rider was Henny Thornton.

"Ruth sent us looking for you," the boy said.

"Trouble?" Fargo asked.

"Sort of. Armstrong. Ruth will tell you," Ritchie said, and put his horse into a gallop.

Fargo followed, the other youth drawing up behind. When they reached Ruth Larkin's, Fargo saw the small knot of figures outside—Aaron Highbard; Dennis Toolan and his wife, Elsa; two young, lean men beside them; and the elder Thornton.

Ruth came forward as he dismounted. "Armstrong's gone his way," she said. "Took his herd and four hands and started up through the mountains. He said he wasn't waiting any longer, but we thought it was just more of his grumbling."

"We expected he'd wait for the rest of us as usual," Aaron Highbard put in.

"He's a damn fool," Fargo said. "When did he leave?"

"Yesterday morning," Ruth said.

"That means he's had nearly two days," Fargo said with disgust. "Time to get into the low range."

"Meaning what?" Ritchie Thornton asked.

"Meaning the Cheyenne won't let him get much higher. Meaning he's going to get himself killed. Meaning he's a stupid fool," Fargo rasped.

"Go after him," Ruth said with her eyes sweeping the others. "Stop him. Save his stubborn hide. He's

125

one of us. We've always helped one another. This is no time to stop."

Fargo's chiseled handsomeness stayed masked as the others exchanged glances and turned their eyes on him.

"What do you think, Fargo?" Ed Thornton asked.

"I don't believe in throwing good money after bad," Fargo answered.

"Meaning we could get ourselves killed trying to save him," Ritchie Thornton said.

Fargo nodded grimly. "Your decision," he said.

"If you caught up to him in time, you could save his hide?" Ruth said, her eyes on Fargo.

"Maybe," was all he'd allow her.

"It's him, the men he took along, and all his cattle. I say we should try," Ruth said to the others.

"There are five of them. I'll take Ritchie, Dennis, and one of his hands. That'll make nine of us. That's a fair posse of guns," Aaron said, looking at Fargo for agreement.

"Yes, if the Cheyenne only want to hit and run. No, if they figure to do more," Fargo said.

"You scouted the lower range. You know how he'd have to go. Will you take us?" Aaron asked.

"I'll take you," Fargo muttered calmly, and pulled himself onto the Ovaro. "Let's move out. Time's important now." He saw the gratefulness in Ruth Larkin's eyes as he turned away and sent the Ovaro into a trot.

The others followed, catching up to him as he headed over the first low hill. The trail of hoofprints was clear, wide, and easy to follow, and he kept a fast pace into the foothills. Armstrong had taken the wide trail that led invitingly up into the foothills, Fargo saw as the hoofprints marched upward in a crowded swath. It would only last for a few hours, Fargo knew.

Then they'd have to break the herd into smaller units. Fargo pushed the Ovaro forward along the trail and continued the hard driving pace until he slowed to a halt as the wide path ended and turned into the three narrow passages that roughly paralleled each other.

Armstrong had sent his herd up each of the passages, Fargo saw, a cowhand bringing up at the rear of each unit. Fargo took the center passage, rode hard up the steepness of it until night lowered itself. He turned off into a place where brush and longleaf pine made a campsite. The others were quick to sleep, and when morning came, Fargo kept the hard pace. Aaron and the others rode with determination. Fargo could only ride with a grim foreboding inside himself. Armstrong had taken an old elk passage when the three paths ended, herded the steers into the narrow strip that went erratically sideways up to the top of the low range. Fargo remembered that it ended in a wide, high plateau surrounded with rock and tree cover, and he rode with his lips drawn tight.

The sun grew high as his eyes swept the terrain, and he cursed the silence inwardly. It was too quiet, the kind of silence that came when wild creatures took cover.

Aaron came up alongside him and sent a quick glance his way. "We've been riding hard. We ought to be catching them pretty soon," the man ventured.

"I'd guess so," Fargo agreed.

"Don't hear any shooting. That's a good sign," Aaron said, and sought agreement in his glance. He received none as Fargo rode on with his intense, handsome face chiseled as if of stone. Aaron fell back with the others.

Fargo peered forward along the uneven trail. He slowed the Ovaro's pace and cast another glance at the sun. It was time for the trail to open onto its end. He'd been following for most of the day, and the upper range loomed just ahead. He moved around a sharp jog in the trail and saw the half-dozen steers lined up along the path. Fargo reined to a walk as the others caught up to him.

"Stragglers," Aaron said. "The rest of them must be just ahead."

"No stragglers," Fargo muttered, drawing a questioning glance. "You hear anything?" he asked. Aaron frowned back. "You hear the herd? You hear any sounds? You know a herd moving along makes a noise—hooves, mooing, bodies rubbing together. They rumble their own special sound."

"True enough," Aaron said.

"We're close enough to hear it," Fargo said, and he moved the pinto forward past the steers along the passage, past another dozen steers standing in knots of twos and threes. The end of the elk trail came into sight, flattening out, and he saw another half-dozen steers. He prodded the pinto forward to the end of the trail and out into the plateau. Two figures lay facedown on the ground just ahead of him, each with enough arrows in him to resemble a porcupine.

"Oh, God," he heard one of the others murmur as they came up behind him. He moved forward, saw two more men crumpled near a rock at the side of the plateau. He moved his eyes slowly forward until he found Armstrong's burly form. The man lay alongside his horse, one foot still caught in the stirrup, his rifle still clutched in his hands. A half-dozen arrows rose from his thick body, one almost all the way through his neck, another with only the feathers and the tip of the shaft visible from where it had gone into his abdomen. "Good God," he heard Aaron Highbard breathe beside him. "Good God."

"Close-range arrows, some of them," Fargo said.

"They brought him down, then came up close and pumped more arrows into him."

"Why?" Aaron asked, the others coming slowly up to stare aghast at the scene.

"Message," Fargo answered. "Exclamation point with feathers. Stay out." His eyes lifted and scanned the rocks and tree cover that looked down on the small plateau. Nothing moved, and he cursed under his breath. "Listen carefully," he said. "Two of you round up what's left of his herd right around here and drive them back onto the elk trail. Do it nice and slow."

"You think they're watching?" Dennis Toolan asked.

"I know they are. This didn't happen more than an hour ago," Fargo said, his eyes sweeping the trees again. "Nothing moves up there. Not a grouse, a partridge, not a deer or a jay. They're up there, and everything else is holed up."

"Why don't we just hightail it?" Ritchie asked.

"Taking the steers might send a message back, sort of slinking away with our tails behind our legs, no threat left," Fargo said. "If it doesn't, they'll be coming for us, and I want to be on that elk trail first with what's left of the herd." He watched Aaron and Dennis Toolan's hired hand peel off and begin to round up the steers as he began to back the Ovaro to the mouth of the elk trail. Ritchie Thornton and Dennis Toolan followed him to where he halted at one side of the trail.

Fargo's gaze continued to sweep the trees and rocks as Aaron and the hired hand began to move the fifteen or so steers. They'd taken most of them into the trail and they had begun to pick up the others along the way when Fargo caught the movement of the trees to his right. He saw the double line of bronzed horsemen begin to descend, slowly at first, then with a sudden rush and shout.

"Into the trail," he shouted at Ritchie and Dennis, and he saw Aaron and the hired hand turn to look back. The steers were a wall of hide and bone blocking any flight down the trail, but he'd expected that. He swung from the Ovaro, dropped to one knee in front of the cluster of steers, and the others followed him. "We'll be damn small targets against the steers," Fargo said. "Wait till they charge in and start firing."

He brought the big Sharps to his shoulder and had it aimed at the mouth of the trail as the Cheyenne raced in. His first two shots toppled two bronzed forms from their ponies. Aaron and the others sent a hail of concentrated firepower at the entrance to the trail, and Fargo saw at least four more Cheyenne fall. The others milled for a moment, then wheeled and retreated.

"Move back slowly, stay against the steers," he ordered, and backed down the trail until he was close by the rear of the herd again. He had the Sharps up again as the Cheyenne appeared, made another charge, and reined up sharply as the hail of lead hurtled at them. They turned and raced out of the trail, and Fargo rose to his feet.

"Mount up," he said. "They won't be back."

"How do you know?" Aaron questioned.

"By the way they came at us," he said. "You can tell how serious an Indian is by the way he attacks. They'd done their real attacking earlier. This was a hit-and-run, chance for a few more dead white men, not worth a major effort." He put the rifle back into its saddle holster and swung onto the Ovaro. "Get the steers moving down," he said. "There's nothing else left here."

"What about a proper burying for Armstrong and the others," Ritchie Thornton asked.

Fargo nodded soberly. "You want to go back and do it?" He saw the young man swallow and turn away. Ritchie Thornton had grown older in the harsh way this land made a man age. "Move them down," Fargo said, and watched the others begin to drive the steers down the trail. They picked up another dozen along the way, and Fargo rode tail, his lips drawn thin. Maybe twenty-five, thirty steers, he grunted. A damn high price for being a damn fool.

They'd be another day at least before getting back, maybe two. He couldn't wait that long, not with Blythe on the rampage. She wouldn't sit still. She'd be readying something, taking some kind of action, and he rode with a sense of foreboding. It was night when they reached the end of the elk trail, and he waited till morning to take his leave. "I'm going on ahead," he said. "You can make it from here by yourselves. Just follow that wide trail when you reach it."

"When will you come by Ruth's place?" Aaron asked.

"Soon as I can. Anybody gets too impatient again, remind them of Armstrong," Fargo said. He turned the Ovaro and sent the horse into a gallop, and the grim foreboding inside him increased with the horse's every long stride.

8

He reached the twin cottonwoods in late afternoon, dismounted at once, and scanned the ground as only he could scan it. He saw no signs that Avery had been there looking for him, certainly none that she had come and waited. Yet he couldn't be absolutely certain. The grass cover was thick and fresh, and it'd had enough time to spring back and obliterate marks. He unsaddled the pinto as night fell, and he took his bedroll into the brush and went to sleep dissatisfied.

He was in the saddle again with the early morning, and he rode into the low hills, through the thick trees into the lush area where the little shack was hidden away. When he neared the clearing, he slowed to a walk, halted as he came into sight of the shack, and swung from the horse. He saw no one, but Abel had remained inside on his every visit unless Avery brought him out. Fargo waited, listened, heard nothing, and let his gaze travel around the edges of the hollow before he stepped forward. Quick, long strides brought him to the open doorway of the shack, the Colt in his hand. He gazed inside and felt the muscles in his jaw grow hard.

Abel lay on the floor on his back, clad only in trousers, sightless eyes staring at the ceiling. A jagged hole in the side of his temple, caked with dried blood, marked the spot where a bullet had entered. But Fargo noted the other marks on Abel's face and body, discolored places, bruises and cuts. Abel had been beaten, perhaps tortured. They'd made certain his poor, vacant mind hadn't revealed anything before they killed him—this time once and for all.

Fargo stepped into the shack, turned over clutter, and halted behind the straight-backed chair. He bent down and ran his fingers across the floor under the chair and felt the crumbs still there. Not the usual amount he'd seen Abel drop, field mice no doubt having eaten most. But enough remained to tell him that Avery had been there with biscuits while he was still alive.

Had they caught her with him? Did they take her off and kill her someplace else? The questions whirled inside him as he rose to his feet and strode from the cabin. He leapt onto the Ovaro and put the horse into a canter. There'd been no other signs of a struggle in the shack, no bits of torn blouse or ripped skirt, and Avery wasn't the kind to go along without a struggle. He rode hard and made himself hope for the best. Blythe would have to be cautious about Avery. She couldn't just have her killed under Howard Simmons' nose.

Fargo was still wrestling with thoughts when he reached the Simmons place in midafternoon. He rode onto the distant hillock that let him peer down at the spread with some safety. He strained his eyes as he gazed at the distant ranch and saw the usual ranch activities. But he spotted the four men with rifles cradled in their arms who were standing along the front of the house. Two of the men strolled back and forth, but the other two were unmoving, positioned directly under the window of Avery's room. It was a good sign in a backward sort of way. Maybe she was being held at her father's house, but at least she was alive and well then.

Fargo watched awhile longer and then backed the pinto from the hillock. He found a little glen nearby, dismounted, and sat down as night came. He waited another hour and then rode back toward the ranch and the line of trees that extended close to the main house. As he had once before, he left the Ovaro in the trees and moved closer on foot. But this time he went into a deep crouch when he neared the main house, avoiding the four guards still in front, and made his way around to the rear of the house. He halted, sank to one knee as he saw the lone figure in front of the rear door.

Fargo frowned as he saw too much open space between himself and the guard. He could edge a few feet closer and then the man was sure to see him. But it was dark, the moon behind low clouds. He'd be only a dark figure until he was right up to the man. He crossed to the side of the house unseen, paused, and straightened up. He'd use another kind of surprise and hope it worked. He rounded the corner, walked slowly, confidently, toward the guard. The man spotted him and brought his rifle around at once. "Hold it there," the man said.

"It's me," Fargo said. He saw the man's head move forward as he tried to peer through the darkness.

"Who's that?" the guard called, uncertainty in his voice now.

"Howard Simmons," Fargo answered, and kept moving confidently forward. He saw the rifle lower a fraction and the man continue to peer forward. Almost abreast of him now, Fargo waited a moment more, saw the man peer at him and his eyes suddenly widen. But realization came too late for the guard as the barrel of Fargo's Colt smashed into the side of his head in a flat arc. Fargo caught the figure as it collapsed and lowered the man to the ground. He stepped over the man, tried the door, and it swung open. He glanced down at the prostrate figure again. The man would stay unconscious a good while, he decided, and he stepped inside the dimness of the house, closing the door after him.

He moved along a short hallway that turned into a long corridor dimly lighted by the glow of lamplight in rooms at the far end. He crept forward when he heard the voices from a room at the end of the corridor, Avery's first, bitterness in her tone.

"How could you?" he heard her say. "I'm a prisoner, your own daughter's a prisoner in her own home."

"Now, Avery, it's all for your own protection," Fargo heard Howard Simmons answer placatingly.

"Like hell. It's for Blythe. She told you to do this, and you're doing it," Avery flung back. "Why, dammit? Why does she want me held here?"

"I told you, she's afraid there's going to be trouble with the small ranchers. I am, too. We don't want you riding around on your own. There's no telling what they might do," Simmons said.

"So you keep me a prisoner with guards outside my window," Avery snapped.

Fargo heard the apologetic shrug in Simmons' voice. "Blythe thinks it's best this way."

"And you just go along with whatever she says," Avery snapped.

"Ed agrees, too. Just trust us, Avery," the man said.

"Trust Blythe Donnen? I'd rather trust a diamondback," Avery said.

"You've the wrong attitude, Avery," Simmons said.

"And it's going to get worse," Avery returned, and Fargo heard her leave the room and rush up the stairway. The exchange had answered a few questions. It was simple enough to figure what had happened. Blythe, suspicious of Avery, had put a watch on her. They'd tailed her to the shack, stayed back, and waited till she left, then moved in to find Abel. Avery was obviously unaware of any of it. Maybe Simmons was too. Whatever reasons Blythe had given him to put a guard on Avery had been accepted with the same willingness he accepted everything else Blythe told him.

Fargo moved forward, slipped into the half-open door of a room as he heard footsteps in the corridor. He crouched in the darkness, smelled the odor of books and leather, and knew he was in the study or library. He listened to the sounds from outside and heard Simmons exchange words with someone else and continue on down the corridor. The house finally grew silent except for the slow, measured footsteps that moved along the corridor every few minutes. When they passed again, Fargo poked his head from the study door and saw a guard with a rifle move on. He watched the man turn at the far end of the corridor and disappear from sight into the other wing of the house.

Fargo rose on the balls of his feet, moved on silent steps to the stairway, and bounded up to the second floor of the house. His hand closed around the knob of the door to Avery's room, and he turned it slowly, noiselessly, and slipped into the room. She had a tiny candle glowing on a night table beside her bed, and he saw her sit up, awake, her eyes finding him. She swung from the bed, a nightgown clinging to her slender figure, flew across the room and into his arms.

"Oh, God, am I glad to see you," she whispered. "How did you get in?"

"Rear door. Convinced a feller to let me in," Fargo said.

She stayed against him, her high breasts firm through the thin nightdress, and suddenly she pulled away, embarrassment in the quick glance she gave him. "I'm sorry," she said.

"I'm not," he answered.

"I couldn't get away. Something went wrong. Blythe's grown suspicious of me," Avery said.

"I know. You were right about her," he said.

"You got the proof you wanted," Avery remarked, and he nodded. "I've got to get out of here. It's been four days since I've been to Abel. I've got to get him some food," she said.

"No, you don't," Fargo said softly, and watched her gray eyes focus on him with sober alarm. "They followed you to the shack," he said.

"Oh, my God," Avery whispered as her eyes continued to search his face.

"They finished the job," Fargo said. Avery turned away, her lips pressed hard against each other. His hand pressed her shoulder gently. "Not your fault," he told her. "Maybe it was hopeless with Abel, anyway." She continued to stare into the dimness, and Fargo walked to the window. He frowned as he saw only the two figures directly under the window. "What happened to the other two?" he murmured.

"They patrol inside after dark," Avery said.

"Get dressed. Take extra clothes. I'm getting you out of here," Fargo said, and watched her walk to a closet. She glanced over at him. "Dress," he said as he continued to stare out the window. He heard her shedding the nightdress, pulling on clothes, and when he glanced back at her, she had put on Levi's and a tan shirt. She stuffed clothes into a small sack as she glanced at him.

"We'll need your roan," he said.

"This'll never work," she murmured, and his glance went out the window again. The stables were diagonally across from the house, some fifty yards back, and he gave the two guards below another quick glance before he turned to Avery.

"You do your part, and I'll do the rest," he said. "You're going to buy time and distraction for me." She nodded and listened gravely to him as he spoke in quick, terse sentences. When he finished, she went to the door, opened it, looked down the dim corridor, and walked to the stairs. She paused, turned, and beckoned to him. He came out, the sack she had filled with clothes over his shoulder, and followed her down the stairway. He cut away from her as she started for the front door. He darted down the hallway on silent steps, ducked into a room as one of the sentries appeared and strolled along the corridor. Fargo waited, listened to the man's footsteps recede, and darted back into the corridor to the rear door.

He slipped outside, stepped over the still-unconscious figure in front of the door, and went into a crouch. He paused when he reached the corner of the house, waited until he heard the voices.

"I'm sorry, Miss Simmons. You can't come out here," he heard the man say.

"Nonsense," Avery answered crisply. "Are you telling me I can't get some air on my own ranch?"

"Not without word from your pa, miss," Fargo heard the other sentry answer.

"He's asleep, and I feel like some air," Avery returned. "I certainly can't run anywhere with you two here watching me, now can I?"

Fargo peered around the corner of the house. She

138

had the two men with their backs to him, and he saw one half-shrug. She was playing her part to the hilt. He saw her start to turn her back on the two men and stroll away. They began to follow reluctantly, and Fargo streaked across the ground, keeping low as his long legs churned through the night.

"Miss Simmons, you can't do this. We'll have to take you inside," he heard one of the man call to Avery. He shot a quick glance across the ground and saw they were still following her as she strolled away. He saw her halt as he reached the stable.

"But I'm not going anywhere," he heard her say as he slipped into the stable. A lone lamp burned low against one wall, enough to cast a dim light that helped keep the horses quiet. Fargo found the roan quickly, in the second stall, the horse's saddle on a peg outside. He led the horse out, saddled it, and climbed onto it, walking the horse to the stable door. He leaned over in the saddle, opened the door just enough to let him see out. Avery had walked back to the front door of the house. Hands on her hips, she was still arguing with the two guards, placing herself so that their backs were toward the stable.

Fargo pulled the stable door open and sent the roan out into a full gallop in split seconds. The men whirled, jaws dropping in surprise as they saw the roan charging toward them. They started to bring their rifles up, but Fargo's Colt spit flame, and the man on the right dropped his gun as he spun and clutched at his shoulder. The other one's shot plowed into the ground as he pitched forward, doubling in two with the force of the bullet that slammed through his stomach.

Avery was running, and Fargo swerved the roan toward her, reached down with one arm, and swept her up as he came alongside her. He felt her clutch his waist as she swung legs over the horse and into the saddle behind him. She held on, arms around him, legs pressed against his hips as he sent the horse full out through the darkness. The sounds of shouts and doors slammed followed, but he was out of range and into the trees when the first shots rang out. He sent the roan through the trees and reined up sharply when he reached the Ovaro, swung onto the horse from the roan, and motioned to Avery as she took the reins. He sent the Ovaro north, streaked across the flatland as she raced close behind him, and didn't slow until he reached the San Juan foothills.

He halted in a little hollow of tanbark oaks and dismounted. "They won't be coming this far," he said, and began to unsaddle the Ovaro. Avery took care of the roan and he set out his bedroll and watched her sit down against a tree trunk. "You've been quiet," he commented.

"I hate running away like that, hate all that it means," she said.

"That your pa takes orders from Blythe?" Fargo said, and she nodded angrily. "You knew that," he said.

"It hurts to have your nose rubbed in it," Avery said.

"You wondering if he knows about Abel?" Fargo asked.

"No," she said too quickly. "That's all her doing."

"Maybe," he said gently, and saw her eyes glare at him. She pushed to her feet, walked a half-dozen paces away, hands clenched at her sides, her back to him. "I'm going to get some sleep," he said, and began to pull off clothes. She threw a glance back at him, turned away at once, keeping her back to him as he undressed to the bottoms of his underwear and slid into the bedroll.

"Not facing things can be a bad habit," he commented quietly. She stayed with her back to him. "You going to stand there all night and get yourself cold again?" he said.

She turned and walked toward him. "Getting into other people's bedrolls can be a bad habit," she said, her gray eyes smoldering.

"Could be. Not facing things is worse," he said, and he slid to one side of the bedroll as she dropped to her knees and swung under the top. He watched her pull the blouse off and shift and wriggle the Levi's off as well. He felt his brows lift as she sat up, turned to him, high, firm breasts very round and perky in shape, with small, pink tips centered on small, equally pink circles. She half-turned, came against him as the top of the bedroll slipped down, and he saw her very round little rear sticking up into the air, her firm, young back and slender, shapely legs. She lifted herself on her elbows, her eyes on him, peering hard.

"This is what you wanted, isn't it?" she almost accused.

"Depends," Fargo answered.

"On what?"

"On what reasons you've got," he said.

"Reasons?" She frowned. "You didn't ask her for reasons, I'll bet."

"You're different," he said calmly.

"Compliments?" she bit out.

"Maybe."

"Why are reasons important to you all of a sudden?" she pressed.

"They're not. They're important to you," he said. "It's important you know why."

Her lips formed a half-pout as she peered at him. "I want to forget everything," she said.

"Anything else?" he questioned calmly.

. "I want you, dammit," she flared.

"That's better." Fargo grinned. "It's called facing things." He half-turned, flipped her onto her back almost roughly, and took in the small rib cage, the flat abdomen, slender, nice legs that stayed tight together, and a small but tightly curled triangle. She had the figure of a young woman, budding, yet full, a combination of sweetness and sensuousness.

Her arms encircled his neck and her lips parted to meet his mouth, and he was surprised at the speed with which her tongue darted forward, hungrily, eagerly. Avery pushed her smooth, slender body up against his. He pulled from her lips to take one firm, high breast into his mouth and tasted the smooth sweetness of it, the tiny pink tip blossoming, lifting, growing firm under his caresses.

"Ah, yes, oh, oooh," Avery murmured as he sucked on the firm breast, just large enough to take almost fully into his mouth, and more little murmurs of pleasure fell from her lips. His hand moved down across her rib cage, caressed the flat abdomen, and moved down through the tight curl of the black triangle. Avery's slender legs lifted as one. His hand went down, closed around the tip of the pubic mound, and pressed between her thighs. He rubbed gently, pressed deeper, and felt her thighs separate a fraction.

"Want to wait?" he asked gently.

She said nothing, but pushed her breasts up to his lips again, and he pressed his tongue down on one tiny tip. His hand stayed and her thighs parted a fraction. He pressed deeper, brought his hand up against the dark warmth of her soft lips, and Avery gave a half-scream, brought her thighs tight together around his hand. He waited, moved gently with one fingertip, touched the edge of the lubricous portal, caressed the slippery softness.

"Oh, oooh," Avery cried out, and her legs fell open, closed, fell open again. He moved inside her, and she cried out with new pleasure, her pelvis twisting, lifting, and he felt her hands digging into his shoulders.

"Take me, Fargo . . . oh, God, please take me," she murmured in between gasps of pleasure.

Fargo stayed half over her, let his hand caress as Avery lifted, quivered, her flesh demanding satisfaction. Slowly, he lowered the throbbing, seeking organ over her little pubic mound, pressed it into the tight curls, and Avery gasped out again. He let himself find her, probe slowly into the warm wetness, and Avery moaned, a soft breathy sound that gathered itself into a scream as he pushed slowly into her.

He felt her slender legs close around him, and the firm breasts lift upward, seeking his lips. He bent down and drew one into his mouth. He pushed deeper into her, drew back, pushed again, began to stroke through the soft wetness with long, slow motions. Her thighs relaxed and tightened with his every stroke, clasped and unclasped around his hips, and he heard the gasped murmurs that were half-pleasure, half-pleading.

"Yes, yes, oh, yes," Avery said breathlessly, and her hands began to dig deeper into his back. A long shudder ran through her body, came again, and again he felt her hips lifting as her hands came up, pulled his face hard against her breasts. "I—I—I'm coming. Oh, more, more, oh, please," he heard her muffled cries. He increased his slow strokes, drove deeper and quicker, and Avery's eyes opened, stared at him, and he saw the gathering inside the gray orbs, almost a wild panic.

He drew back, thrust hard, quick, short, fervent strokes now, and Avery's voice grew into a wild wailing sound, a prolonged paean of pleasure, and he felt her body tightening around him, inside and out, lips and legs, contraction and constriction. She stayed, clung to that moment of climax, unwilling to let it slip away, her mound pushed hard against him, thrusting upward, continuing to thrust, encompassing all of his exploding maleness as her wailing cry rose skyward.

The wail snapped away with a sudden, short burst of sound that was made of despair, a cry within a cry, and her legs fell away from him and her slender, firm body grew limp. He slid down with her, staying inside her as her breathing softened and her arms relaxed around his neck. She murmured an unhappy sound as he slid from her and lay beside her. She curled around him, one leg over his legs, and stayed there as she fell asleep almost at once. She clung to him with hardly a change in position as he finally closed his eyes in sleep. She was still hard against him when he woke with the morning sun.

She stirred, opened her eyes sleepily when he slid from beneath her and pushed from the bedroll to pull on trousers and gun belt. His eyes swept the sur-roundings with a slow glance. "Stay put. I'll be right back," he said, and walked into the trees, following his ears to the soft bubbling of a small mountain pool fed by an underground spring.

He returned to the hollow and pulled Avery to her feet, led her beautifully naked to the little pool, where the morning sun flecked the water with yellow specks. He put the Colt and the gun belt down on the grass within each reach and stepped into the little pool. Avery followed and let out a little yelp at the coldness of the water. He closed his arms around her and dived down into the pool. Avery stayed with him and shook herself as they surfaced. She slipped away and swam on her back, the high, firm breasts pushing up from the surface of the water.

He floated, letting the cold, bubbly water clean and refresh him before finally pulling himself out onto the grassy edge of the pool. When Avery stepped out, the tiny nipples were standing firmly erect, droplets of the cold water still clinging to them. She lowered herself beside him and pushed the little, firm nipples into his chest, pressed herself against him, and her lips found his, a sudden, eager burst of wanting in her kiss. Her hand came down along his still-wet body to find his organ responding at once, thickening, rising.

Fargo gathered the smooth wet body against him, took her again as he answered the explosion of her wanting until her wailing cry of ecstasy drifted into the warm sun and she lay beneath him on the grass, slender legs still encircling his waist. Finally, they slid down his thighs and she lay satisfied and clinging beside him. He let her half-sleep until she stirred, sat up, and stretched. He enjoyed the sight of her slender loveliness as the firm, young breasts lifted pertly.

"What happens now?" she asked, suddenly growing all seriousness. "Do we pay the land survey office a visit tonight?"

"Yes, but I'm thinking we won't just walk in," Fargo frowned.

"Why?" Avery asked.

"Blythe knows about you and Abel now. She knows you might suspect a connection, even though he didn't tell you anything," Fargo said. "I'll wager she's put the place under guard by night."

"So what do we do?" Avery asked.

"First, I'm going into town to take a look at the place," Fargo said as he rose, pulled her up, and walked back to the hollow.

"It's a small, one-story building in the center of town," Avery said. "There's a side entrance."

"I still want to have a look for myself," he said. "You'll be safe here till I get back."

She nodded as he dressed. When he finished, her arms slid around his neck. "Be careful," she murmured.

He patted her firm little naked rear. "Get dressed," he said. "I don't want any distractions when I get back." She watched him ride off with a satisfied smile, and he took a direct route back until he neared the Simmons ranch, where he made a wide, skirting circle, and reached Mountainville a little after noon. He rode slowly down bustling Main Street and spotted the land survey office quickly, the name in gold on a sign hanging outside the door. Avery's description had been accurate, but it was the houses and the street across from the building that held his attention. He surveyed the two frame structures, one holding a barbershop and an assayer's office, the other a dry-goods shop. They'd all be closed down by night, he grunted as he rode past and circled back again. A narrow alleyway about eight feet wide separated the two buildings, he noted, and he finally turned the pinto and headed away from town. He had just come abreast of the general store when he saw Blythe mounting the dark bay. Three men plainly waited for her to one side, and her eyes darkened as she spotted him.

She moved the dark bay toward him, and her face had become a beautifully icy mask. "You've your nerve coming into town," she hissed.

"Can't see why," Fargo answered mildly.

"I know that little bitch didn't get away from her father's place all by herself," Blythe said through

146

hardly moving lips. "It was you who helped her. I'd bet on that."

"You're just still feeling frustrated, honey," Fargo said.

"Bastard," Blythe Donnen said. Even in fury, her alabaster skin didn't color, he noted abstractly. "And you're a fool. You could've had so much," she snapped.

"Yep, everything but self-respect." He smiled.

Blythe Donnen's eyes grew smaller. "You'll have a pine box to put all that self-respect in, Fargo," she hissed.

"I figure you've got one all picked out for me," he said, and smiled again as he tipped his hat and rode on slowly.

She passed him at a hard canter, the three men following her. He let her hear his laugh. He rode from town, his eyes sweeping the land, practiced glances seeking signs of company. But there were none. Blythe had gone on, and he rode alone back across the low hills, finally reaching the San Juan and the little hollow in the late afternoon.

Avery leapt to her feet as he rode in, rushed to him with her gray eyes filled with relief. "God, I was getting worried," she said.

"I'm fine," he told her. "Mount up. We've some visiting to do."

She turned, swung onto the roan, and followed him without questions as he started back toward town again but swung west when he reached the flatland. They reached Ruth Larkin's place as dark began to settle. The woman hurried from the house, surprise in her face as she saw Avery.

"I'll need five or six men," he said. "Can you get them here fast?"

Ruth Larkin nodded and turned to Jess. "Go to

Aaron's place first, then to the Thorntons', and Sam Dunstan is just down the line from there," she said, and Jess ran behind the house, appeared again racing an old gray into the dusk. "It'll be about a half-hour or so," Ruth said, turning back to Fargo, and her eyes flicked at Avery as the younger woman slid from the roan.

"This is Avery Simmons," Fargo introduced.

"I know who she is," Ruth Larkin snapped irritably, and threw a frown at him.

"I told you somebody has been helping you," he reminded her, and saw the woman's mouth fall open, her stare go from him to Avery and back again. He nodded slowly, and Ruth Larkin pulled her mouth closed and met Avery's eyes.

"Why?" she asked. "Your pa's been trying to do us in."

"Blythe Donnen's been trying to do you in," Avery corrected.

"He's part of it," Ruth said.

"He's just another kind of victim," Avery answered. "She's evil. She has my father under her domination. We have the same enemy with different reasons."

Ruth Larkin studied Avery for a long moment. "I think I understand," she said.

"Figured you would," Fargo injected.

"What's that mean?" Ruth frowned at him.

"Women understand some things right away," he said, and received a quick glare from Ruth before she turned to Avery.

"Come inside and wait," she said. "I want you to know I'm beholden for whatever you've done for us."

"I wish it were more," Avery said as she followed the woman into the house and sat down at the kitchen table. "It's all blown up suddenly," she said.

Ruth served mugs of hot tea, and Fargo sipped the

brew as he sat long-legged in a too-small chair. "It's coming down to the wire," he said. "You'll be driving cattle in a day or two."

"You want to tell me where?" Ruth said.

"Not yet," Fargo answered. "I can only promise one thing: it's going to be the hardest drive you'll ever make. You tell the others to call up whatever hands they figure to use. You'll be needing every hand, every horse, and every gun."

"You decide to go through the mountains?" Ruth asked.

"I decided to lead a cattle drive," Fargo answered.

Ruth made a face at him and glanced at Avery. "He never gives you the answers you want to hear," she said.

"How true." Avery sniffed, and Fargo rose to his feet as he heard the sounds of hoofbeats outside. He was waiting beside the house as Sam Dunstan and his son rode up, Aaron Highbard close behind them. Ed Thornton and Henny followed soon after. They dismounted and gathered around him as he sipped the mug of hot brew.

"We're going into town when midnight passes," he said. "The land survey office. I expect there'll be at least four guards in front, maybe six. The stores across from it will be closed and dark, and there's an alleyway between the two buildings. You'll have plenty of place to take cover."

"Take cover and do what?" Ed Thornton asked.

"Keep those guards busy firing back at you. You sweep by first, lay down a first volley, and then take cover across from the office and keep firing. You don't have to hit any of them. I don't care if you do, but the important thing is for you to keep firing. Keep them busy. Stay back, don't risk your necks, and keep firing at them."

"While you get inside the survey office," Aaron said.

"Give the man a cigar," Fargo said. "One thing more. You've a sheriff in town, I take it. Would you go to him if I find something rotten?"

The others exchanged glances.

"I wouldn't," Ruth Larkin said. His glance questioned. "His name's Eddie Grayson. He got the money to run for election from Blythe Donnen and the combine," she explained.

"He's their man, owned and locked up for them," Aaron Highbard said.

"Enough said," Fargo answered.

"How long do we keep them busy outside the office?" Aaron asked.

Fargo glanced at Avery. "I can find the records in minutes if they're there," she told him.

"You heard her," Fargo said, and Aaron peered at her.

"How does she fit in here with us?" he asked sharply.

"She fits. Ruth will explain. We'll start ahead. You get there anytime past midnight. The town will be asleep by then," Fargo said as he handed Ruth the mug and went to his horse.

"All that shooting's bound to bring the sheriff," Ed Thornton said.

"It'll wake him, but he won't go running into a pitched gun battle. He'll wait till you stop firing. And you'll be off and gone when that happens," Fargo said. "One more thing: I want everyone here tomorrow morning, every rancher there is."

"I'll see to it," Ruth said as Fargo rode on with Avery. He sent the pinto into the darkness, and Avery drew alongside him, her face grave.

"What if you don't find anything?" she asked. "What if everything's in order?"

"Can't be," he said tersely. "Abel knew something. It's got to be in that office."

"What if it isn't?" she persisted.

"I'll get to that when and if I have to," he snapped, and she fell silent as they neared the town. He slowed the pace and guided the horse along the back edge of the town until he halted across from the survey office, now dark and still. "You stay here. I'm going to have a closer look," he said, and moved the Ovaro forward past the rear of two buildings to his right. He turned and steered the horse between them through a narrow space. He halted at the edge of Main Street, dismounted, and inched his way to the corner of one of the structures where he could peer down the street. He swore silently as he counted the figures positioned across the front of the land survey office. Four strung out against the building and one more at the head of the passageway alongside. He backed the Ovaro down the narrow space and rode slowly back along the rear of town to where Avery waited.

"Sometimes it's best not to be right," he muttered grimly. He sat silently, waited, and when he saw the moon lift itself high above the buildings, he swung to the ground. "Get your little ass down here, honey," he said. "It's time to go find answers.

"Maybe." She sniffed as she climbed down to the ground beside him. He knelt on one knee and drew the Colt from its holster, felt Avery alongside him. He caught the sound of horses first, hard-riding hoofbeats and, moments later, an explosion of gunfire. It took only seconds for the guards to return fire as they hit the ground.

Fargo listened to the momentary lull as Aaron and the others took cover across the street. And when the

151

gunfire erupted again in a furious volley, he rose to his feet. "Let's go," he flung at Avery as he sent long legs driving across the ground toward the rear of the building. He darted into the passageway alongside, skidded to a halt at the side door, and yanked at the knob. "Goddamn, it's locked," he rasped.

"Of course," Avery said tartly.

He glanced up the passageway. The man that had been there had vanished, and the hail of gunfire continued. Fargo put the Colt to the door, fired, and the lock blew apart. It was but one more shot amid the others, and he pushed into the office, stood aside for Avery to enter, and pulled the door closed. Despite the near-total darkness, he saw her move forward with surefooted steps and followed her dark shape. She halted abruptly, and he bumped into the edge of a desk as she found a lamp and turned it on low.

"In here," she said, and pulled at the deep drawer at one side of the wooden desk. The drawer stayed closed and Fargo came around to the front of the desk and brought the butt of the Colt down at the lock on the drawer. The lock held, and he had to smash two more blows against it before it finally splintered away.

He yanked the drawer open as the exchange of gunfire still sounded outside, and Avery pulled a sheaf of file folders out, emptied them on the desk, and frantically rifled through the pile of claim sheets. "Here," she said, holding a half-dozen long claim sheets up, and Fargo took them from her hand, spread them out on the desktop. He scanned the sheets in the glow of the lamp, his eyes moving quickly down the stiff, stilted phrases of official forms. He turned the first claim over, finished the paragraphs on the back of it as he searched to find something out of order. There was nothing, and he went through the other two claim sheets. They were exactly like the first, only the name at the top changed.

"Dammit," he muttered.

"I told you they were in order," Avery said, and Fargo's lips drew tight as he read the claims again. Blythe Donnen's first, Simmons' next, and Ed Sowerby's last. Each was an official form awarding them the rights to the vast stretches of land they claimed. His fist slammed down on top of the desk as the hail of gunfire continued outside.

"I can't see it. I can't find it, but there's something," Fargo rasped. "I know it. I feel it, dammit." He turned from the claim sheets and yanked at the other drawers of the desk. They all came open at once, each filled with more file folders, papers, survey forms. He slammed them shut and returned to the claims on the desk. "Only this one drawer was locked. That means something," he said. "The answer's got to be in these claims somewhere." He started at the top of the first claim sheet again, Blythe Donnen's, and cursed silently as the minutes ticked away. He heard the hail of gunfire outside began to taper down. Aaron and the others were breaking off the barrage. The five minutes were over. But his eyes stayed riveted on the official forms in front of him, his gaze burning into each line.

"We're out of time," Avery whispered, and he shook his head in agreement as he continued to stare at the claim sheets. He started to pull his eyes away when he stopped, felt the explosion of excitement erupt inside himself. "There, goddammit," he rasped. "It's right there in front of me. Only it's not there."

"Are you all right?" Avery frowned. "You're not making any sense."

He picked up the top claim sheet and waved it at her. "Look, no file numbers, no stamp," he said, pointing to the bottom corner of the form as Avery continued to frown at him. "Every claim officially filed has a file number on it and an official stamp," he said excitedly.

"What are you saying?" Avery asked.

"I'm saying these claims were never filed. They were drawn up in this office, everything proper, everything in order, except the file numbers and the stamps because they were never sent on to Washington. That's what Abel knew. That's what he was going to bring into the open. That's why they tried to kill him."

The last shots ended, and the silence was abrupt for a long moment, and then the sound of voices, cursed shouts, and running footsteps.

"We've got to get out of here," Avery whispered, and blew the lamp out. Fargo took her hand, dodged around the desk after her as she found her way to the side door. He pushed out first, whirled as he saw the figure step into sight at the front of the building. He fired, too fast, and the shot missed, but the man dived out of sight. Fargo ran, pulling Avery along with him, his long legs racing across the ground behind the building. Avery slipped, half-fell, and he yanked her up and pulled her along. They reached the horses, leapt into the saddles as a handful of wild shots followed.

He rode hard, stayed at a full gallop until he reached the low hills and found a spot under a wide-branched hackberry. He dismounted as Avery slid wearily from the roan. "This'll do for what's left of the night," he said. "They'll be too busy checking things out and sending for Blythe to go chasing the country-side."

Avery slumped to the ground, her gray eyes filled with questions as he came down beside her. "What does it all mean? I don't understand it. Why didn't they file the claims?" she asked.

"Those claims gave them control over huge stretches of land, the major route into New Mexico. They knew the government wouldn't accept claims for that much land. That bothered me from the very first," Fargo explained.

"Then they don't own the land," she said.

"That's right, except for their own ranchlands. They don't own any of the rest—not Blythe, not Ed Sowerby, and not your pa," Fargo said.

"How do they expect to go on holding land they know they can't claim? It doesn't make sense," Avery said.

"Ah, but it does, if you understand how these things work. A man holds a piece of land he doesn't claim. If he holds it long enough and everybody accepts it as his, it becomes his in actuality. When he finally files a claim, another set of factors come into play. He adds the right by use to his claim. It makes it almost certain to get a claim approved then. It's not a question of disapproving a new claim any longer. It becomes a matter of taking away land a man has used, worked, held on to for a long-enough time, land the community has accepted as his. A right-by-use claim usually goes through because the government simply accepts what has been an established fact, whether they're happy about it or not."

"So they have to hold the land long enough and keep everybody thinking it's really theirs, until they think it's time to file a right-by-use claim," Avery concluded.

"Right." Fargo nodded. "Anybody who insists on seeing the claims will see those properly filled-out forms, signed by Thomas Boyard of the land survey office. Nobody's going to even notice that they don't have file numbers or an official stamp attached."

"And anybody that does, Blythe will take care of in her usual way," Avery said. "But this means that Boyard is in on the deal too."

"Yes. I'm sure he's being paid off properly and stands to make more in time," Fargo said. He reached out, took Avery's hands in his. "Your pa's a part of the scheme, honey. He has to know about the fake claims, the squeeze on the small ranchers to make sure they accept the combine as owning the land. You've got to face it."

"All right, he knows all that. Blythe has talked him into it. But that doesn't prove he knows about killings, kidnappings, about Abel, or any of the other things she's arranged," Avery said.

"No, it doesn't," Fargo conceded. "But it's getting harder to believe that."

"Not for me," she shot back.

"No, not for you," he agreed gently, and pulled her to him.

She came at once, her lips lifting to his, seeking instant refuge. "Make me forget it all again, Fargo," she said. "This one more time before tomorrow comes."

He pressed her down onto the soft, cool grass, and his hand found one firm breast. "Before tomorrow comes," he murmured.

"Oh, oh, yes, please, please," Avery whispered, pulling at the blouse almost frantically. She shed clothes as he did, and her slender, lovely warm smoothness came over him, the tiny, firm nipples pressed hard into his chest, her legs moving up and down along his body. She rubbed her little triangle over him, across the rising, answering maleness of him, and little sounds of pleasure came from her lips.

He felt himself rise, come erect, and Avery lifted, wriggled, sank down on him, and her cries of delight spiraled into the still dark.

"Oh, oh, yes, yes," she said as she began to move up and down over him. He let her have her way, watched the firm, pert breasts rise and fall, her head go back as she arched over him, drove herself harder and harder onto the spear of pleasure. When she felt the moment exploding, the climax of ecstasy rushing over her, she fell forward atop him, pressed her breasts into his face, and her cry resounded in his ear. She stayed on him, legs pressed tight, her slender form shaking against him until she finally went limp over him, almost collapsing onto his muscled frame. She stayed there, not moving until he finally slipped out of her, and she straightened her legs, slid from him, and curled against him.

She slept at once, unwilling to allow even a fraction of a second for thoughts of tomorrow to creep in. Perhaps it was best that way, he reflected as he closed his eyes beside her.

9

He arrived at Ruth Larkin's soon after morning came, Avery on the roan beside him. Aaron and the Thorntons were there, and the others arrived soon after. No one had been hurt during the night, he was glad to see. "You did real well," he said to the men.

"We followed your orders, just kept sending lead their way," Aaron said. "You find what you wanted?"

Fargo nodded and began to explain, his words terse, short, setting down all the facts. He heard the murmurs of surprise turn to anger when he finished.

"The lyin' bastards," Ed Thornton growled, and his eyes went to Avery. "Sorry, young woman, but I can't hold back words because of you."

"I don't expect you to. I understand how you all must feel," Avery said.

"They've been fooling us all along, swindling us, too," Thornton said.

"But this means we can drive right across the land without paying the bastards," Sam Dunstan said.

"Only this time they'll be out to stop you," Fargo cut in. "With bullets instead of fake claims. Blythe Donnen's hired gunslingers, I'm sure, and by now she knows I'm onto the whole scheme. She has no choice but to stop us, wipe out every last one of us. We'll be outgunned and trying to drive a herd of cattle. How many of us will there be?"

"Eleven men, twelve with you, Fargo," Thornton said.

"Thirteen," Avery put in quietly.

"Fourteen," Ruth Larkin added. "Jess can stay here and look after the calves, and I'm a good shot."

"Four to always ride herd. Ten to fight. We'll still be outgunned, but we'll have to make do," Fargo said. "The important thing is that we can't just let them come at us when they're ready. We can't be sitting ducks for them."

"Hell, that's all we can be. There's no hiding place out on the plains," Pat Hennessy said.

"We'll make our own hiding place," Fargo said, drawing a round of frowns. "Get to your herds. Take pieces of brush and long branches and tie them onto the tail of every damn steer, hanging down long enough to scrape the ground. Out past the good grass, the ground is pretty bare and dry. We're going to make ourselves a dust cloud big enough to hide us all. You start getting your steers ready, and I'll explain the rest later. I want to start driving through this afternoon. I don't like to keep anyone waiting."

"We'll have the herds together and ready just south of Mountainville in two hours," Aaron said.

"I'll be there. Everybody bring extra kerchiefs and extra bullets," Fargo said as he spurred the Ovaro on. Avery followed him as he rode slowly across the low hills and halted atop a gentle rise, his eyes sweeping the land below. "You're not coming," he said softly.

"The hell I'm not," Avery snapped instantly. "I'll pull my weight."

"I can't see you shooting at your pa," Fargo said.

"There'll be plenty of others to shoot at," she returned. "You expect he'll be there?" she questioned.

"He might," Fargo said.

"Then he might be shot. I want to be there if that happens. You can't deny me that," Avery said. "I've a right. I've earned that."

Fargo let a long sigh escape his lips. "Yes, I guess you have," he conceded. "But you better keep your blond head down."

She leaned over in the saddle and brushed his cheek with her lips. "I will," she said. "So I can keep it down the next time we make love."

"Best reason I've heard so far," Fargo said, and moved forward.

"You think Blythe will be with them?" Avery asked.

"I'd guess she'll hang back and watch, let her hired guns do the work," he answered. He rode on slowly, stopped, and cleaned his Colt, and the time passed quickly enough. He saw the herd as he drew near across the flatland. He rode slowly through the herd, his gaze taking in the branches and brush tied to each tail. The dust was already beginning to rise as they swished tails, and he rode to where the others waited. He went over the rest of his plans, making certain everyone understood, and cast a glance at the sky. "Move 'em out," he said. "Onto the dry ground. I expect we'll have a few hours before they come at us."

He pulled to one side as the others began to circle the herd and slowly drive the steers forward, out beyond the thick grass first, and then south. The herd picked up speed as they moved straight across the flatland, and Fargo stayed off to the side as the others held the steers in tight. The spiral of dust began to rise at once, growing thick quickly. At the end of the first hour it was a dense blanket that followed the herd. By the end of the second hour, it was a gray cloud that had spread to cloak all but the very outside edge of the herd and the riders who moved back and forth with shouts and the slapping of leather.

The herd continued to move well, and the dust cloud grew heavier and lower as it settled over the steers, feeding on itself as more dust rose with every few hundred yards of trampling hooves. He sent the Ovaro forward ahead of the herd and Avery rode with him until he reined to a halt. He nodded to the line of horsemen that had appeared directly ahead of them, spread out in a single line. He counted twenty riders as he called back to the herd. "Keep them moving," he said. "Straight ahead." He turned, watching the herders move back and forth on the outside of the thick mantle of dust that hid almost every steer now.

He stayed to the side and watched the dust cloud move forward. The line of horsemen peeled away to form two groups and break into a gallop. "Hold your places until they get closer," Fargo called to the others, and drew the Ovaro in nearer to the herd. He watched the attackers come in on both sides of the herd, letting them draw near. When the first shot rang out, he sent the Ovaro into the cloud of dust, Avery beside him. He pulled a kerchief over his mouth and felt himself rub against the steers. He reined back and used the sense of feel to let the horse move the steers forward.

A volley of shots exploded and ended, and he heard the shouts from outside. "Son of a bitch, I can't see anything," a voice said. "No sense in wasting good bullets on a dust cloud."

"Keep riding alongside," another voice shouted. "Tell the others to ride alongside."

Fargo's smile was a thin line. The herd was moving along well in the dust cloud. He could feel the pace as the Ovaro went along. He pushed the kerchief from his mouth for a moment. "Anybody near?" he called out.

"I am," Avery answered.

"Over here," he heard Ed Thornton's voice answer, muffled in the dust.

"Just keep the herd moving along. It's going fine," Fargo said. "Pass the word. Just keep moving."

"Got it," the man said, and Fargo pulled the kerchief over his mouth again. He let the Ovaro walk with the steers, the horse's presence helping to keep the steers moving forward, and caught the voices from beyond the cloud of dust.

"You can't hide in there forever, you stinkin' bastards," someone called, and punctuated the words with a shot fired in frustration.

"Take it easy," someone else shouted. "They're not gettin' away. It'll be dark soon and they'll have to pull up. When they do, that dust cloud will lift and we'll be right here waiting to blow them away."

Fargo's hard smile stayed under the kerchief. The voice outside was absolutely right. The dust cloud would quickly begin to shred and blow away when they stopped. The cool night wind would hurry the process, and a man on horseback sat too high for steers to hide. The attackers would see each target outlined under the moon as the dust cloud disappeared. Except for one thing, Fargo grunted grimly: there'd be no horsemen outlined, no riders jammed amid the herd, immobile and easy targets. He kept the Ovaro moving along with the herd and felt the steady wavelike motion of the herd as the others stayed among the steers. The dust let him see nothing but grayness, but suddenly the grayness began to darken. The night had begun to slide over the prairie. He kept moving on with the steers for another half-hour, and the dust had become a black shroud as hooves still stirred up more of the impenetrable blanket.

He pulled the kerchief from his mouth again finally, his voice strange-sounding as it drifted through the dust-laden air. "Who's near?" he asked, and Avery answered first again, somewhere ahead and to his right.

"Over here," he heard Ed Thornton answer to his left, and then Dennis Toolan from somewhere in back of him.

"It's time," he said. "Stop the herd. Let them settle down. You know where to go from there. Pass the word." He listened to the other voices, muffled sounds as they passed the word to those nearest and they in turn called it out to still others. It was going according to plan, and he slowed the Ovaro, pulling the horse to a halt. The others were doing the same, he knew, and as the horses came to a halt, the steers rubbing against them slowed and halted, those riders at the head of the herd doing the major job. But he felt the motion of the herd begin to slow, finally halt, a long, gradual stopping not unlike the motion of a long wave finally coming to rest. The sound of soft bellowing rose up in the thick, dust-filled air as Fargo turned the Ovaro sideways and let the horse act as a further block to the nearest steers.

He stayed in place, counted off minutes, and listened to the herd settle itself. The thick blanket of dust acted as a calming influence as the steers, unable to see out, huddled together protectively. Fargo pulled one leg over the saddle finally, pulled the kerchief from his mouth. "Avery," he called softly, and she answered almost directly in front of him. "Time," he said as he dropped to the ground and made his way along the steers, using his hands to feel along the warm fur. He felt a breath of wind and knew the dust cloud was already beginning to shred. He made his way between steers, brushed past wet noses and switching tails, received more than one hard push from a flank that moved sideways. But he could see the edge of darkness now as the dust began to lift. He glanced across the trailing edge of the dust cloud, saw Avery, Ed Thornton not far from her, two more shapes beyond him.

He pushed through the last of the steers that formed the edge of the herd, and dropped to the ground just past the line of sharp-edged hooves. He began to crawl forward, into the clear air of the night, stayed flat on the ground, and turned his head to take in the line of figures that also lay flat. He saw Avery nearest to him, Ed Thornton next, Ritchie nearby, and the others impossible to recognize. Another line of prostrate figures emerged crawling from the other side of the herd, he knew, and he kept himself pressed hard against the soil.

The dust cloud was disappearing quickly now, only errant wisps left. Fargo saw the line of horsemen come into view as they headed for the herd. One of the riders in the foreground raised his arm. "Blast 'em, every damn one of them," he called out as he sent his horse into a gallop.

Fargo brought the big Colt up, took careful aim. The line of attackers raced forward, the riders peering into the herd, trying to spot the horsemen amid the steers. They never looked down as they charged forward, never saw the line of figures prone on the ground. The Trailsman fired the first shot, a bead drawn on the lead attacker, and the man flew from his horse as if he'd been yanked off by invisible wires as the heavy slug slammed into him. A fusillade of shots erupted from the line of fires beside him, and Fargo saw the attackers topple like so many ninepins.

The shots exploded from the other side of the herd at almost the same instant. He aimed at another of the horsemen as six of the remaining riders began to peel away. He fired, and another attacker went down.

Avery was firing furiously, the others alongside her, and he saw three more of the horsemen fall. The last two turned their horses and raced away. Only one made it into the night as he fired a final shot. Fargo rose on one knee, listened to the last flurry of shots from the other side of the herd, and pulled himself to his feet. It had gone exactly as he'd planned, and it had been finished in a matter of minutes. The safe shroud of dust first, then the complete surprise as the attackers charged in with blind, arrogant confidence.

He saw the others getting up, Avery already standing. She moved tentatively toward the figures that lay scattered on the ground, pausing to peer down at each. He walked to her as she reached the last cluster; she turned to him, her gray eyes wide with cautious hope. "He's not here," she said.

"That's good," Fargo answered.

"He could be on the other side," she ventured.

"He could be," Fargo agreed, and fell silently into step beside her as she made her way around the herd. He saw Ruth standing next to Sam Dunston's boy as they came around to the other side, Pat Hennesy nearby. "Everybody all right here?" Fargo asked.

"Mike Hennessy has a nick on one arm, but he's all right," Ruth answered. Avery was already moving among the figures that lay lifeless across the ground, and he followed after her, paused for a moment beside one, and then went on. She had reached the last figure and turned to Fargo as he came up.

"He's not here," she said.

"Ed Sowerby is," Fargo said.

"Yes, I saw," Avery said tightly. "Pa must have stayed back with Blythe."

"Seems that way," Fargo agreed as he turned away and walked to the others. "Let's clean up around here and bed down," he said, and Lemuel Dunstan and three of the others helped him drape the still and lifeless figures across their saddles. The horses were then run out into the darkness.

Aaron chose two men to tend the herd for the first shift. Fargo put his bedroll out a few yards away and watched Avery pull her bedroll near, yet far enough away to be proper.

"What now, Fargo?" he heard her ask in a half-whisper.

"Sleep," he said curtly. "See what tomorrow brings."

"You expect another attack?" he heard her ask in alarm.

"No, they're finished," he said. "Good night, dammit."

"Good night," she murmured, and he let himself sleep quickly as only the distant howl of a Mexican red wolf broke the night silence.

He woke with the prairie sun to find Pat Hennessy and Dennis Toolan gone and Ruth Larkin up and about. "They went to bring the chuck wagon. It's a long drive to Albuquerque without one," she said.

"You won't be needing me to break trail now. You know this route well," Fargo said.

"No, we won't, but you've earned your pay twice over. Aaron will be taking care of that," she said. Her brown eyes held his, and the morning sun gave her plain brown hair a tinge of copper. "I'd still like it if you came visiting," she said, and the unsaid lay in the dark brown of her eyes.

"Maybe I can," he said, and turned away as the others began to get up. Avery had risen, ran her hands through her blond hair with quick motions. Ruth had brought a sack of biscuits and bacon that she passed around, and Aaron came to Fargo with the roll of bills.

"Money's not enough for what you did for us," he said.

"Enjoyed doing it," Fargo said, taking Aaron's handclasp as he watched the horseman come into sight in the distance. The lone rider approached, and Fargo stepped forward as the man neared and reined to a halt.

"Avery Simmons," the rider said.

Avery stepped forward with a frown. "Yes?" she answered.

"Your pa sent me. He says to come home. It's time to talk. He's waiting for you," the man told her.

Fargo saw the tiny, pleased smile come to Avery's lips. "All right," she said softly.

"I'll take you back," Fargo said.

"He said she should come alone," the man put in quickly.

"Why?" Fargo frowned.

The man shrugged. "I'm just deliverin' the message. That's what he said, she should come alone."

"Tell him I'll be there," Avery said, and the man turned his horse and left.

"I'm going with you," Fargo said as Avery glanced at him.

"No, I'm going back alone. That's what he wants, and I can understand that," she said.

"It's a damn trap," Fargo said.

Avery's chin tilted upward defensively. "Nonsense. It's over now and he wants to repair fences, maybe explain a lot of things."

"I don't like the smell of it," Fargo said.

"You're always suspicious. Blythe's run off. You'll see. She's gone, and he's realized what she is," Avery said.

"No, not her, not yet," Fargo growled.

"Why do you say that? Running is all that's left for her," Avery said.

"No," Fargo said stubbornly. "Maybe not for him either."

"You've never really understood about him, how she had him hypnotized. Besides, he wouldn't call me back into some trap. That's ridiculous," Avery snapped.

Fargo grimaced inwardly. Trust and love were hard things to fight, and she clung to both with eager desperation. He watched her walk to where the roan grazed on a patch of grama grass. "I have to go. It'll be night before I get there," she said, and swung onto the horse. She paused a moment before him. "Will you come by soon?"

"Yes," he said, and watched her ride across the prairie until she was a tiny dot on the horizon. He turned and bumped into Ruth Larkin at his elbow.

"You'll be going after her," the woman said with a tiny smile in her eyes.

"You seem sure of that." Fargo smiled.

"I am," she said.

"Why?"

"Because you know about men and women, women like Blythe Donnen and men like Howard Simmons," Ruth said. "Good luck," she added as she strolled away.

Fargo smiled after her and watched the others begin to gather in stray steers as they prepared to move on. He stayed, waved them on as they left. He wanted to give Avery plenty of time to get ahead of him. The trip was mostly across the flat prairie land,

and he didn't want her to catch sight of him following. She'd stop and argue more and refuse to let him go with her. Staying far enough back was best, and the Ovaro could make up time when it came necessary.

He let the sun rise almost into the noon sky before he mounted up and sent the horse at a steady pace over the prairie. It was late afternoon when he met Dennis Toolan and Hennessy driving the chuck wagon back. They exchanged waves as he hurried by. He reached the hills at dusk, increased speed, and had covered the low, lush rolling countryside when night fell. He slowed as he neared the open expanse of the Simmons ranch and guided the pinto into the single line of trees that stretched almost to the house. There were lights on in the main room of the house, and he dropped to the ground, leaving the horse and continuing forward on foot. He headed for the rear door of the house. He was getting to know the way real well, he reflected, but this time there were no guards, no one at all patrolling the grounds.

He slipped into the house and heard the voices from the large living room at the far end of the corridor. He edged forward on the balls of his feet, past the ajar door of the dark study. He inched still farther and stayed against the opposite wall of the corridor, which let him see into the living room at an angle.

"You said we were going to be alone," he heard Avery's voice accuse.

"I said for you to come alone," Howard Simmons corrected. "Blythe thought that would be best."

Fargo inched forward, dropped to one knee where he could see into the large room. Howard Simmons stood beside a small table, Avery nearby with her back to the door, and Blythe Donnen faced her, tall, commanding, her black hair and alabaster skin still as striking as ever. Fargo's gaze stayed on Blythe for a moment and saw she was entirely composed, cold confidence in her face. Avery's voice grew angry as she turned to her father.

"You're still going along with what Blythe thinks best? After all she's done? I don't believe you," Avery threw at him.

Blythe's voice answered. "Howard loves me, don't you, dear?" she said with a smile that barely avoided condescension. Howard Simmons' silence was its own answer. "And he understands that whatever I did was for us both," Blythe said.

"Hah!" Avery snorted. "You never did anything for anybody but yourself. You're a murdering, lying rotten bitch."

"*Avery!*" Simmons thundered. "You've no right to talk like that."

"My God, you're blind, more blind than I thought possible," Avery flung back at him. "I know the things she's done to make her swindle work."

"And you're not going to tell anybody anything," Blythe interrupted. She wore a long black skirt with a tailored white blouse, and as Fargo watched, she drew a short-barreled tranter percussion pocket revolver from inside the skirt. English-made, it was a five-shot, double-action gun capable of blowing a good-sized hole through its target despite the compactness of it.

"Blythe, what are you doing?" Fargo heard Simmons gasp. "You said we'd just all talk and try to make up."

"Shut up, Howard," the woman said, her voice suddenly made of ice. "I can't afford to have this little turncoat bitch daughter of yours running around loose. Neither can you, whether you know it or not."

"Put that away, Blythe, this minute," Simmons said, and Fargo heard him try to bring authority into his voice. He started to come around the little table.

"Stay there, Howard," Blythe ordered, and he stopped.

"Blythe, put that away," he said, his voice turned into a plea.

"Shut up, Howard," Blythe snapped again, and the pistol stayed unwaveringly on Avery. Fargo drew the Colt. He'd heard enough. He took one long step that brought him to the doorway. He let the click of the hammer sound as he pulled it back.

"Drop the gun, Blythe," he said, the Colt aimed at her from the doorway. "I can't miss at this range."

Avery spun, took a step sideways as she stared at him with her gray eyes wide. There was nothing between him and Blythe Donnen now.

"Drop it, honey," he growled. "This Colt shoots faster than that thing you've got. I'll have two bullets in you before you get that trigger back."

"I don't think so." Blythe smiled, and Fargo stiffened as he felt the hard end of a rifle barrel push into his back. "Drop the gun, you big bastard," she said.

Fargo cursed silently as he let the Colt fall to the floor, and the man with the rifle stepped around him, keeping the gun pointed at him. He was the man that had brought the message to Avery, Fargo saw, and he swore at himself again for not being more careful. The man had probably been hidden in the study he'd passed. Fargo brought his eyes back to Blythe and saw the little smile of satisfaction on her face.

"I thought if I got her here I'd get you, too," she said. "You followed her, just as I expected. Fools and protectors, one and the same." She laughed.

"You can't do this, Blythe. What's come over you?" Simmons said, his face chalk white.

"Say good-bye to little Avery, Howard. I haven't

171

any more time to waste," the woman snapped, and brought the pistol up.

"No, my God, no, Blythe," Simmons shouted.

Fargo saw him dart forward at her, arms outstretched. Blythe Donnen shifted the pistol a fraction and fired. Avery's scream pierced the air as Howard Simmons fell back against the little table and slid to the floor. Avery rushed to him as he lay against the table, one hand clutching his stomach as he groaned in pain.

"Oh, God, oh, Daddy ... Daddy. Oh, my God," Avery cried out as she cradled her father's head in her arms.

"It's all right, my little girl," Fargo heard the man gasp. "It's all right."

"Leave him," Blythe Donnen ordered sharply. Avery ignored her, and Fargo saw the woman take a step forward, grasp a handful of blond hair, and fling Avery half across the room. "I said leave him," she shouted. Fargo's eyes went to the man with the rifle. He was a foot too far away to reach without getting shot. "Outside," the woman ordered. "I want you two dead outside. It'll look as if someone had come in to rob the place and there was a running gunfight."

Fargo measured distances to the man again and once more decided the odds were against him. He waited as Avery stumbled toward him, caught her arm, and helped her outside. The rifleman kept the gun trained on him as he stepped into the front of the yard.

"You, over here," Blythe ordered as she waved the pistol at him, and Fargo stepped to the side. "Now, you over here, you interfering little bitch," she snarled at Avery, and motioned to the hitching post.

Avery backed to the end of the post. Fargo swore in

helplessness as the rifle stayed dead on him. He watched Blythe raise the pistol, and take aim.

"Think of how nice it'll be, you and your protector lying almost side by side," the woman said.

Fargo heard the shot explode and felt his lips pull back. His eyes on Blythe, he saw her mouth fall open as she took a half step backward. And as he watched, one alabaster-white breast turned red. He spun around and saw Howard Simmons, one hand clutched to his bloodstained midsection, the gun in the other hand. As he stared, Howard Simmons fell forward to the ground. Avery rushed to him, and Fargo's eyes went to the man with the rifle. Equally taken by surprise, he still stared at Simmons as the man lay on the ground.

Fargo moved with the speed of a cougar's strike and lunged forward. The man tried to bring the gun around, but he was too slow, and Fargo's hands closed over the gun. He twisted, using the power of his huge shoulders, and the rifle tore from the man's grasp. The man half-stumbled back, terror in his eyes. "I was just followin' orders," he said, but his hand reached for the six-gun at his hip.

Fargo fired, and the figure seemed to bounce along the ground until it lay still. "You follow the wrong orders, you end up in trouble," he murmured, letting the gun fall to the ground. He turned and saw Avery push herself to her feet and fling herself into his arms.

"He was bewitched," he heard her sob. "Bewitched."

"He broke the spell," Fargo murmured. "For you."

He led her to the roan and took her into town. She told him where she had a friend there. She clung to him when he left her there, sobs without sound now.

"Will you come back?" she asked.

"Not likely," he told her honestly. "What will you do?"

"Stay on. Try to run things the way they used to be run. Maybe throw in with the small ranchers," she said.

"You'll work it out," he told her, and she pressed her lips to his, a gentle echo, and ran inside before he rode on. He turned the Ovaro west, rode slowly over the low hills and made a detour. The lone red cedar loomed up in the moonlight and he halted before the house as Jess Larkin came out.

"Howdy, Fargo," the boy said happily.

"Tell your ma something for me, Jess," Fargo said, and the boy nodded. "Tell her my visiting never worked out. But tell her I wanted to."

"Sure, Fargo," the boy said.

Fargo nodded and rode into the night. Ruth would understand the words he'd left. He could almost see the little glint of satisfaction in her eyes. The world was made of knowing and doing, and sometimes it was enough just to know.

LOOKING FORWARD!

**The following is the opening
section from the next novel in the exciting
Trailsman series from Signet:**

THE TRAILSMAN #54
KILLER CLAN

---

*1861—Fort Larned and points west,
where a dark-haired siren lures unsuspecting travelers
into the blood-soaked bosom of a mad family*

Fargo pulled his pinto to a halt and gazed across the undulating swath of grassland at the hotel and the cluster of buildings around it. Built of peeled logs and raw lumber, the unpainted structures stood out gauntly in the bright, late-afternoon sun. At first glance it seemed pretty damn foolish to build a hotel in the middle of an empty sea of grass. But just beyond the hotel Fargo could see the rutted, sun-whitened trace of the Santa Fe Trail. According to Fort Larned's Commanding Officer, this hotel was perfectly situated to serve as a supply depot and a much-needed resting place for the steady stream of settlers using the trail on their way west.

From where he sat his pinto, Fargo picked out a general store, sheds, two small barns and a large horsebarn, with an abundance of corrals in back for stock. In the corrals, Fargo glimpsed good solid

Missouri mules, some oxen, and horses, saddle stock and work horses. The tallest structure was the hotel, three stories high, dominating the small compound.

Fargo nudged his Ovaro off the saddleback and kept to an easy lope as he traversed the long grassy swale fronting the cluster of buildings. He was doing his best to contain his sense of urgency. If Lieutenant Becker was not off his feed, the two men Fargo had been seeking for the past six months were staying at this hotel, waiting to join a wagon train that would soon be passing the hotel on its way to Santa Fe.

As Fargo pulled his pinto to a halt before the hotel, he saw a long-necked gent step out of a barn to peer at him from under the brim of his straw hat. He was carrying a pitchfork and was dressed in filthy bib overalls. At the same time a round, cheery-looking woman, hastily wiping fresh flour off her hands, came out of the hotel door. Halting on the hotel porch, she beamed at Fargo.

"I'm Mrs. Clemm," she cried. "Welcome! Welcome! My land! It's so good to see a friendly face!"

Dismounting, Fargo dropped his reins over the hitch rack. "Thank you, ma'am," he replied, looking past her at the hotel.

Despite its roughhewn exterior, the hotel impressed him. The walls were solid, the windows spacious, and the veranda fronted the entire length of the building, its roof serving as the floor of a railed balcony.

A chunky, powerful-looking fellow stepped out onto the porch. Looking at them both Fargo found their resemblance to each other uncanny. No question about it. They were mother and son. The young man smiled broadly at Fargo, like someone trying to imitate the village idiot.

"Howdy, mister," he said heartily. "You sure are a welcome sight after that crazy Indian."

"What Indian?" Fargo inquired. He had seen no sign of one on his way across the prairie.

"He was just here an hour ago," said the young man. "We saw him watchin' us from that saddleback. Been there all morning. Ma gave me a blueberry pie to bring out to him—a kind of peace-offerin'. But when I rode out, he galloped away. A crazy-lookin' devil he was, wearing a red-shirt and breech clout."

"Well, bless me," said the little round woman. "There's no sense in worryin' about that savage now." She beamed at Fargo. "I'm Ma Clemm and this here's my boy, Matthew. You can call him Matt."

"Name's Fargo," Fargo returned. "Skye Fargo."

"My, what a lovely, poetic name!" Ma Clemm exclaimed. She turned to her son. "Ain't that so, Matt!"

"Yup," said her son solemnly, "it sure 'nough is."

By that time the tall man who had stepped out of the barn on Fargo's approach had pulled up alongside Fargo. He had been joined by another young man carrying a pitchfork.

"Pa—Aaron," Ma Clemm cried happily, "this here's Skye Fargo. An' he's come to room with us for a spell. Ain't that right, Mr. Fargo."

"Reckon so. If you've got a room for me."

Pa Clemm nodded solemnly to Fargo, then removed his hat to wipe off his face and neck with a filthy polka-dot handkerchief, revealing a skull as bald as a doorknob. Rawboned, with a lantern jaw, long, scrawny neck and eyes sunken into deep hollows, Pa Clemm resembled an ambulatory skeleton decked out in bib overalls and clod hoppers. His son Aaron bore a spooky resemblance to his father—only on a larger scale. His outsized, lanky figure rippled with powerful muscles, and his face, though almost as gaunt as his father's, was strong and powerful, the eyes peering out at Fargo from under beetling brows.

"We've got a room, sure enough," replied Pa Clemm. "Hell, we've got more'n one. We got plenty." He grinned suddenly, revealing very large, black teeth. "Things've been a mite slow."

"They'll pick up, though," said Aaron confidently. "We're expecting a wagon train through here any day now."

"Enough talkin' " cried Ma Clemm happily. "Come in, Mr. Fargo! Get yourself settled. You're just in time for supper, Lord love you!" She seemed so delighted at the prospect of his company that for a moment Fargo expected to see her clap her hands like a child.

As she turned to go back into the house, a girl about twenty appeared in the doorway and smiled at Fargo. She was a lush-looking armful with dark coils of hair falling down onto her shoulders, clear past the rising plateau of her firm, upthrusting bosom. She must have been working alongside her mother in the kitchen, since there was flour on the front of her apron and a smudge of it on one cheek. Her dark eyes took Fargo in quickly, and he saw her straighten a bit in the doorway, coming alert the way a poker player does who finds himself filling an inside straight. There was a wet-lipped, tarty looseness about her suggesting to Fargo a damn good time ahead, and though he couldn't be absolutely certain of it, he thought one of her dark, liquid eyes closed in a wink.

"This here's Melody," said Matt, grinning.

"Say hello to Mr. Fargo, Melody," said Aaron, who had been watching Fargo. There was a lewd smile on his face as if he had been reading Fargo's thoughts.

"Hello, Mr. Fargo," said Melody, her voice a husky, teasing lilt.

"You can call me Skye," he told her.

"All right, Skye."

"Here," said Pa, lifting the pinto's reins off the hitch rack. "Let Aaron take care of yore hoss, Mr. Fargo. Boy, he's a right purty one. Indian, ain't he?"

"He's an Ovaro pinto," Fargo told him.

"Forages on grass too, I'll bet," said Aaron, his eyes lighting as he took the reins and surveyed the pinto's powerful, chunky frame.

"He does that," Fargo replied, untying his warbag from the saddle and lifting his Sharps from its scabbard. "Comes in handy on long rides."

"I'll bet it does."

"You ridin' alone?" asked Matt from the porch, as Aaron led off Fargo's pinto.

Ma Clemm disappeared back into the hotel, but Melody stepped all the way out onto the porch and leaned back against the wall, her hands behind her, her bosom and belly thrusting out provocatively. She was wearing slippers, and it didn't appear to Fargo there was much under the one thin, tattered dress but herself. She was appraising him coolly, her dark, almond-shaped eyes glancing boldly at his crotch.

"Yeah," replied Fargo. "I'm ridin' alone."

"You ain't a lawman, are you?"

Fargo was about to tell Matt that this was none of his business, but he didn't want to get off on the wrong foot with this family—especially if the two men he wanted were somewhere on the premises.

"Nope," he replied. "But I'm hopin' to meet up with a few friends of mine who're stayin' here."

"Friends of yours, you say?"

Fargo smiled. "That's right. I heard tell they're waitin' for that wagon train you mentioned."

"Where'd you get that information?" asked Pa Clemm, sending a dark dagger of tobacco juice to the ground.

"The Commanding Officer back at Fort Larned."

"Well, we did have two such guests," Pa Clemm admitted easily. "Lieutenant Becker weren't lyin' about that. But them two ain't here now." He sent another gob of chewing tobacco at the ground. "They rode out."

"When," asked Fargo, doing his best to hide his disappointment.

"Near a week ago."

"I thought they were going to wait for the wagon train."

"That's what they said. Guess they got tired of waiting."

"Which way'd they go?"

"West."

Pa grinned suddenly at Fargo, but his eyes were no longer so friendly. "You say you ain't a lawman, but you're sure enough after them two. That right?"

Fargo nodded wearily. "Maybe you could describe them to me. I might have the wrong ones."

"I can describe them," said Melody, pushing herself away from the side of the hotel and walking to the edge of the porch steps and sitting down on the top step. Leaning back on her elbows, she let her knees swing open slightly and began to describe the two men, her knees edging steadily wider as she spoke.

At the end of her description of the two men, Fargo knew for damn certain sure that Melody Clemm was wearing nothing at all under her dress—and that her description of the two men was complete enough for him to realize that once again he had arrived too late.

"That's them, all right, Melody," he told her.

"Does this mean you won't be stayin' for the night?" she asked, her knees moving apart a fraction further.

"Doesn't mean anything of the sort," Fargo replied, aware of tiny beads of perspiration standing out on his forehead. "I could use a good feed and a good night's sleep."

Melody smiled and got to her feet. "I'll tell Ma to make dumplin's!" she said, as she vanished inside.

Pa Clemm joined Fargo as he started up the porch steps. "You'll be wantin' a bath," he said. "We got a room set aside in back of the kitchen. Finest wash tubs west of the Mississippi. Had them shipped all the way from St. Louis. There's plenty of hot water and soap, and Melody'll wash your clothes for you too. She'll boil 'em real clean."

"Then tell Aaron to bring up my bedroll and saddle bags so I'll have a change."

"Yessir, I sure will, Mr. Fargo."

The hotel lobby was simply a large living room with a small desk in a corner and a stairwell leading upstairs. The walls had no pictures, none at all. And there were no decorations on shelves or standing in corners on tables, nothing to indicate that the Clemm family had a history or a treasurey of memorabilia.

Pa Clemm moved behind the desk, dipped a metal

pen in an inkwell, then turned the register so Fargo could sign. The pages of the register were filthy, their edges yellowed and cracked. Squinting at the last signature, Fargo could barely read it and the date was illegible. With a shrug, he signed, after which Pa Clemm, chattering cheerfully, ushered him into the back room, where rusted galvanized tubs were sitting about waiting for use. If they had been shipped all the way from St. Louis, that must have been a long, long time ago.

Leaving him for a moment, Pa returned to take his clothes, by which time Fargo had stripped down to his long johns. After Pa Clemm left with his clothes, Melody entered carrying a bucket of steaming water. She smiled quickly at him and proceeded to fill the tub, making three trips in all. When it was ready for him, she indicated as much and left the room.

Slightly disappointed, Fargo peeled out of his longjohns and stepped into the steaming water. He splashed about for a while, scrubbing himself with abandon. He was about to step out when Melody returned and proceeded to scrub down his back, twice rinsing it with bucketfulls of hot water. Her hands were quick and warm and thorough and soon the brush she was wielding had peeled off his back a couple of acres of Kansas soil. Then she scrubbed his hair, working it into a fine lather before rinsing it with a stinging bucketful of steaming water.

During all this time, though she worked close enough to him that the sight of her heavy, billowing breasts was enough to give him a fierce, painful erection, she made no attempt to follow up the promise of that wink she had flashed him from the hotel doorway earlier.

Until she was finished.

In the act of wringing out the sponge, she suddenly leaned over, her hand dove into the water, and squeezing his erection in a vice-like grip, she kissed him on the lips, her mouth working like something alive. Before he could reach up to grab her, she was gone, leaving behind the ghost of a laugh as she closed the door behind her.

"Sakes alive!" Ma Clemm cried, her round face beaming. "You ain't hardly scratched that pile of mashed potatoes—and don't forget that pork gravy. If I do say so myself, it's the best I done in a long time. Now go on and eat up, Mr. Fargo!"

Smiling, Fargo reached over for the potatoes; but it was Melody who got it first and handed it to him. As soon as he had placed it down next to his plate, Matthew was handing him the gravy and Aaron the platter of pork chops. Grinning, Fargo hurried to fill his plate. He was on his second helping, but in truth he had never tasted pork chops this good, nor such smooth, delicious mashed potatoes and gravy, not to mention the slabs of thick, homemade bread and the rich, golden butter he was in such a hurry to spread on it. But it was the rhubarb pie Fargo was looking forward to, and he was anxious to leave some room for it.

Melody finished helping her mother and sat down beside him. Earlier, while serving him, she had bent so close her pillow-like breasts had nearly pressed against his face and neck, and he had to force himself not to grab her around the waist, pull her to him and close his mouth over one of her nipples. Now, as he ladled the pork gravy over the steaming mounds of mashed potatoes on his plate, Melody edged her chair closer and rubbed her knee against his thigh. In that instant Fargo realized it was her bare knee he was feeling, which meant she had lifted her skirt up past it. Then her hand dropped casually to her lap and a moment later found its way to his crotch. Fargo almost spilled the gravy over the linen tablecloth.

Melody giggled at his reaction.

Pa Clemm glanced over at them. "Looks like you two young 'uns have hit it off," he said, chuckling. "Saw it first thing. Just you go slow, Mister Fargo. Hear?"

Forking a pork chop onto his plate, Fargo nodded. He was willing to go as slow as the law allowed. The trouble was, he didn't see how he was going to be able to fight off this heated-up she-cat if she insisted. After all, he was only human.

Watching Fargo, Matthew nudged his brother eagerly as he chomped happily on a piece of pork, his round face grinning lasciviously. It was obvious the two brothers knew precisely what Fargo was up against. Abruptly, Melody's hand found its way in under Fargo's pants, and before he could pull away, it closed about his erection. He nearly jumped straight up. As it was, he dropped his fork.

"Now, Melody," cried Ma Clemm fretfully, aware that her daughter was likely up to no good, "I'd thank you to just let our guest eat his supper in peace."

"Aw, Ma," Melody complained, "I was just funnin'."

"You heard Ma," snapped Pa Clemm. "Sit back there now and eat your vittles."

Pouting, Melody pulled back from Fargo and began to eat. Relieved, he reached for another pork chop.

But no sooner had his teeth closed about the succulent meat than Melody's left hand once again closed firmly about his erection—as if it were a handle she was using to keep him close.

"Lord love you, boy!" cried Ma Clemm, placing the new platter full of sliced bread down on the table, "You sure got a good healthy appetite! Does a woman good to see food disappear this fast. You want more pork chops?"

So fervently did Ma Clemm speak on this matter that what Fargo realized suddenly was her wig slipped down over her forehead. She snatched at it quickly, planting it back where it belonged. Looking closely for the first time at her round, cheery face, Fargo saw the course, wrinkled texture of her skin just beneath the powder and rouge she had plastered over it.

"No thanks," Fargo managed. "If I eat another pork chop, I'll likely turn into a pig."

"Well, now, we wouldn't want that," said Matt. He nudged his brother. "Would we?"

"No, surely wouldn't, and that's the truth," replied Aaron.

"You're too nice just the way you are," Melody told Fargo, leaning so close she singed him.

Leaning back suddenly, Pa dropped onto his plate what was left of the pork chop he had just devoured. Wiping his hands on his overalls, he said, "Ma, how about slicin' me a piece of that rhubarb pie while I go get my jug."

"Now, Pa!" Ma cried in some alarm. "No sense in going to that jug this soon. Can't you see we got ourselves a visitor?"

"I didn't say he couldn't join me, did I?" He got up and started off to get the jug, glancing back at Ma as he did so, "Now, you heard me," he said. "Cut me a wedge of that pie."

Obediently, Ma Clemm left the table and went over to the sideboard to slice the pie. At the same time Melody's hand closed about Fargo's rigid shaft as she leaned close to nibble maddeningly on his ear, her hot breath searing him.

With a sigh, Fargo gave up thinking of the rhubarb pie, the hot fragrance of which had maddened him the moment Ma Clemm placed it down on the sideboard.

He had another, fiercer appetite to satisfy.

When Fargo finally left the table, Pa was deep in his cups and Melody was over by the sink, washing dishes. Ma Clemm hurried over to him and lit a candle to lead the way upstairs to his room. He mumbled a good night to the Clemm clan. Grinning, Aaron and Matt waved the pork chop bones they were still gnawing on, while Melody just glanced across the kitchen at him, a look of pure raw desire flaming in her cheeks.

Ma Clemm put the candle down on the nightstand beside the bed, turned down the covers for him, then bid him good night and closed the door firmly behind her. Fargo had undressed and was relaxing on his back, the candle flickering beside him, when he heard the light, rapid knock on his door.

Not at all surprised, he got up and went to the door and pulled it open. Melody glided in swiftly. He closed the door and turned to her. She was waiting for him and flung her arms about his neck and kissed him, holding nothing back.

He pushed her away, his senses reeling. "Your Pa know you're up here?"

"Of course not. He's still nursing that jug and Ma is busy in the kitchen."

"And your brothers?"

"They rode off somewhere. What're you afraid of? Me?"

He smiled at her in some exasperation. "Why wouldn't I be? You almost raped me at the kitchen table."

"It's been a long time since I seen the likes of a man such as you. I'm just a good healthy woman is all. Am I too much for you, Mister Skye Fargo?"

"A man's got to be careful," he told her. "That's all."

"You want me to go on back down to the kitchen?"

Fargo took a deep breath. When the day came he didn't feel up to handling a woman—any woman—he might as well put a bullet through his head. No man could tell what was waiting for him beyond the next hill, but that sure as hell shouldn't keep him from riding over it.

He stepped forward, took Melody's face in his hands and kissed her on the lips—harder than she had kissed him. When he finished and stepped back, it was obvious Melody's senses were reeling now.

She grinned back at him weakly. "Is that your answer?"

"It is."

She plucked at a few buttons, then flung her dress over her head and stood before Fargo stark naked. Her figure was as lush and ripe as a peach in September, with a waist almost narrow enough for him to span with his hands and with powerful hips that flared lushly into thick, powerful thighs. Her pubic patch was as big as a platter and gleamed like a dish of blackberries. Smiling lewdly at him, she moistened her slack, full lips, then shook loose her long dark hair, allowing her curls to tumble clear down to her waist, a few of the dark strands coiling about her large, pink areolas.

It was clear he had another feast in store for himself.

Trying not to show his eagerness, he pulled down his buckskin pants. Before he could stop her, Melody stepped close and stripped off his longjohns as well. Peering at his surging erection, she laughed. Then, pushing him gently but firmly back toward the bed, she clambered atop him, fastening her full, pouting lips upon his with an eagerness that inflamed him. Wrapping his arms around her, he flung her over under him, his powerful chest muscles rippling like a big cat's, his lake-blue eyes smoldering with need for her. Laughing, Melody reached up and ran her fingers through his thick shock of black hair.

"You got Indian blood, ain't you," she said.

"On my mother's side."

"Mmm, I knew it. I like that. You won't just roll over afterward and go to sleep."

He fastened his lips around her nipples and felt them surge upward, swelling with eagerness, becoming as hard as cherry stones. She began to moan. His lips traversed down into the hot, sweaty valley between her snowy mounds, then continued on down to her belly button.

"Go further, Fargo," she pleaded. "Please! Oh, please!"

He obliged. She kicked wildly, plunging her hands through his hair. Grinning, he scooted up onto her. Her great thighs parted eagerly and he plunged his shaft into her soaking mound, surging past her outer lips, grinding in recklessly, without caring whether she was ready or not.

She was ready. More than ready. He began thrusting frantically—his need to climax outracing his control. As he slammed into her repeatedly, she laughed and sucked him still deeper inside her, closing her thighs and finging her arms around him, cleaving him to her with the strength of barrel staves. Her tongue found his neck just under his ear, as he came within her triumphantly.

She felt him come and bucked happily in response. Fargo could not be sure, but it seemed she was coming, also. Panting, he looked down at her.

"That was for openers," he told her.

"It better be," she told him fiercely.

Pulling out from under him, she turned over on the bed and lifted her rear end, showing him the way she wanted it. With a shrug, he obliged.

About half an hour later, she was on top of him, slowly gyrating, bringing him to climax despite his distended stomach. It was amazing what she could bring out of him, and at last lightning struck his groin and he began plunging and rearing furiously, impaling her upon his fiery sword. As he lunged fiercely upward, she keened aloud and flung her head back as she began to come. While he filled her with what little he had left, she continued to pulse and gyrate, her hands reaching down to grab his thick hair while she came again and again. He marveled at her capacity for orgasm and did what he could to keep his erection solid until at last, moaning softly, she flung herself down upon him, tucking her hands under his chest and hugging him gratefully.

A sudden, deep lassitude fell over him—as if he had been drugged. Crooning softly, Melody kissed him about the lips and on his forehead, gently stroking his damp hair back off his forehead. Then she kissed him on the lips, her tongue probing wantonly. But Fargo could not respond. She pulled back and Fargo heard her soft, delighted chuckle.

He was only dimly aware of her pushing herself off the bed and pulling the bedclothes up around him, then stealing softly from the room, her dress tucked under her arm. He heard the click of the latch as the door closed behind her, took a deep breath and rolled over to face the window. On the small nightstand behind him, the candle was still burning, its pale, flickering light casting his shadow on the wall beside the shuttered window. It bothered him. He turned back around to snuff out the candle—and as he did so he remembered something: he was sleeping in a strange bed without a weapon of any kind under his pillow.

This was not how the vigilant Skye Fargo had managed to keep his scalp on for so long.

He groaned, not wanting to move. He was exhausted, totally. But a deep, insistent voice chided him for his foolishness. A woman was one thing, but his life—and the search for those remaining two men—was something he could not risk, no matter how tired he was.

Muttering against the effort it took, Fargo pushed himself upright and stared blearily at the corner where he had piled his gear, the Sharps leaning against the wall, his gunbelt and six-gun on the floor under it. With a weary sigh, he pushed himself off the bed and padded woozily over to the corner, slipped his Colt out of the holster and brought it back to his bed. As he dropped onto the mattress, he shoved the big revolver under his pillow, closed his eyes and was asleep before the mattress stopped moving under him—the candle still glowing on the nightstand beside him.

Like a wild animal, Fargo awoke instantly, every sense alert. The part of him that never slept had heard the sound of a board creaking just outside his door. It had stopped suddenly, the way it does when the person leaning on the board hears it creak beneath his foot and freezes.

Facing away from the door, his eyes on the wall near the window, Fargo kept himself perfectly still and waited. When the sound did not come again, he began to drop off once more and was almost completely under when the candle's flame flickered sharply and Fargo saw the shadow of his head and shoulders wavering on the wall.

Someone had opened the door.

His fingers closing more securely about the Colt's grips, he kept his eyes on the wall. When the door opened all the way, the candle's light danced so violently, it almost went out. The flame steadied, and a moment later Fargo heard a floorboard creaking not five feet from his bed as a heavy, stealthy foot eased carefully down upon it. Fargo counted to five, then flung himself completely around, flinging up his Colt as he did so.

He found himself staring into the startled faces of Aaron and Matthew Clemm. Stark naked, their testicles hanging from their crotch, the two brothers looked like unclean apes, legs bowed, hair wild, their faces livid with the excitement of the hunt—and each one holding in his hand a huge, freshly honed knife.

Behind them, guarding the doorway, stood Pa Clemm, his gaunt face alert as he held in his powerful, bony hands what looked like a crowbar.